*More House*

# *More House*

HANNAH CALDER

Vancouver
New Star Books
2009

NEW STAR BOOKS LTD.
107 — 3477 Commercial Street | Vancouver, BC V5N 4E8 CANADA
1574 Gulf Road, #1517 | Point Roberts, WA 98281 USA
www.NewStarBooks.com | info@NewStarBooks.com

*More House* is a work of fiction, a product of the writer's imagination. Any resemblance by any character to any person, living or dead, is entirely coincidental.



We acknowledge the financial support of the Canada Council, the Government of Canada through the Book Publishing Industry Development Program, the British Columbia Arts Council, and the Government of British Columbia through the Book Publishing Tax Credit.

Cover design by Mutasis.com
Illustration by Roxanna Bikadoroff
Printed and bound in Canada by Imprimerie Gauvin, Gatineau, QC
Printed on 100% post-consumer recycled paper
First printing, June 2009

LIBRARY AND ARCHIVES CANADA CATALOGUING IN PUBLICATION

Calder, Hannah
More House / Hannah Calder.

ISBN 978-1-55420-042-9

I. Title.
PS8605.A456 M67 2009 C813'.6 C2009—900720—7

*For Eva, who was once a boy*

*For spirits, when they please,*
*Can either sex assume, or both; so soft*
*And uncompounded in their essence pure,*
*Not tied or manacled with joint or limb,*
*Nor founded on the brittle strength of bones,*
*Like cumbrous flesh; but in the shape they choose,*
*Dilated or condensed, bright or obscure,*
*Can execute their airy purposes,*
*And works of love or enmity fulfil.*

— *John Milton,* PARADISE LOST

# *Cast List*

| | |
|---|---|
| THE GIRL | Daughter of the girl's parents, lover of many and few, maid, mother of Joey, no-name brand |
| JOEY | Son of the girl, son (on certain pages) of Mrs. Nobody |
| THE LORD | The Lord |
| HANNAH | Cook, witch |
| SOLOMON | Groom, son of Steven, young, young, young, young man |
| STEVEN | Butler, father of Solomon. |
| GRACE, HOLLY & MARIE | Maids, porn actors |
| DEAD WOMAN | Impersonation, makeup |
| THE GIRL'S PARENTS | Borrowed from my mother's imagination |
| HELEN | Childhood friend |
| HELEN'S DAD | Childhood friend's father, the butcher |
| MRS. NOBODY | Joey's mother (on certain pages) |
| MR. NOBODY | Joey's stepfather (on certain pages) |
| MY STEPFATHER | Stepfather |
| MY MOTHER | Mother |
| & YOURS | No pretence here |
| GRANDAD | My mother's father |
| DORA | My mother's mother (resurrected) |
| GRANNY | My stepfather's mother (recalled) |
| MRS. SCHUSTER | Cookery teacher, nemesis |

& various gorgeous animals (visitors)
Guest appearance by EMILY DICKINSON.
The DIRECTOR and her crew, including MY DAD as lighting technician (my dad), ME (the writer), THE EMBROIDERER & THE BOOK.

# 1

Joey sees a woman with the heel of a shoe embedded in her skull. It is her own — a white stiletto, imported from a 1980s music video. Her left cheek rests sleepily on the doorstep. In the poverty-stricken light he cannot tell her genre, but he guesses 'blonde.'[1]

The woman's miniskirt has thrown up its hands in frustration. He sees her euphemism, then a second stiletto — still on its foot. Tall bamboo lines both sides of the path that leads to the tableau. At their tops they fluster with a sinister hush. Fussy leaves.

Joey wouldn't be here on this street if it wasn't for his mother's fear of mice. She let out a scream and there it wavered until Mr. Nobody gathered what was up. There. Up there over the rising potato froth. Beyond reason — for a mouse is no larger than an open mouth, screaming.

Joey wouldn't be here if it wasn't for his mother's fear of her own husband. (Why can't *she* punish him? She's the one who is angry.) Hand poised to spank, Mr. Nobody turns upon his wife's scream and buggers it. Joey, bent over the desk with his eyes crossed, trying to focus on the tip of his nose — a distraction technique — is spared. After Mr. Nobody has left the room, Joey waits an obedient while, then reaches down and pulls his English trousers, or Canadian pants, up.

Passing the kitchen on his way outside he sees his stepfather with a knife, dabbing peanut butter onto a mousetrap. His

1. Correct guess.

mother has left the kitchen to stand on chairs in each room of the house waving her feather duster at spider floss. Click. On sticks for children. And their chins. Does that make sense? OK. Everybody in position.

## 2

People die. Joey's make-believe father, Mr. Radio (who), died in 1977 (when). It was nice, Joey thought, that his dad was the kind of man who would lie on the floor and listen to music, and also, what was the song on the falling radio (how)? The answer to that question is in Mrs. Nobody's mouth somewhere, although logically the song couldn't have played right up until she came home with shopping bags and rolling oranges. So she made it up and fed it to Joey on a teaspoon.

People die. Yes. And not always in movies.

# 3

The woman's name is illegible. It's been smeared. She's a young and pretty slutty slut. Her back hurts from lying on the doorstep and is England-cold up and in the tailbone. She's been borrowed from someone with a good eye; someone able to pull a slag out from a slag-heap. Nothing is as it seems, but as it has been arranged. By the director, myself, a few others. Makeup, especially, have gone to town on her. The blue eye shadow of a teen magazine has broken into chunks and fallen as powdery rain onto the eyelids of our star. She will have a speaking part, but first we must see her dead.

There is something comical about beginning in this way. It looks like none of us have graduated from film school. The budget, tight-fisted and promising to get us nowhere, has no producer to manage it. The director and I are green. I like her only because she has access to a camera. A rich daddy. She's agreed to shoot two movies. One for me and one for her. Mine a pornographic murder mystery; hers a period piece, (which will eventually end up fused together as a pornographic period mystery.) All of our people will double up at least once, usually twice, and get paid for only half the work they do.

I ask Joey's stunt double, who is standing nearby in what seem to be English trousers, if it is really possible to push the heel of a shoe into a person's head, even with the help of a top-notch special-effects team. Even then? He says, 'nope.' I am glad, but not about the fact I need to take this sleeping beauty back to the drawing board.

In miniature, she is easy to carry. The only thing I worry

about is that the sweat on my hand will wash her away, or that she is cold-blooded (who knows anything about the physiology of characters?) and will be burned alive in my palm. Like a worm.

# 4

Director: 'You show me yours and I'll show you mine.'

Me: 'At the same time, OK? One . . . two . . . three . . . GO!'

We slap our wads of nonsense onto the table, brushing fingers during the exchange. Immediately I see that hers is more professional. Better font. Better layout. Disease-ridden with technical jargon: DOLLY SHOT. INT. THE KITCHEN. ANGLE ON.

'What are these things?' I say, pointing at DOLLY SHOT.

'Just ignore them. Look at the descriptions and dialogue only.'

'Actually, I'd rather not,' I say. 'Let's just trust each other and wing it and see what happens. When I've got the camera I've got the camera and when you've got it you've got it and that's it. OK?'

I'm nervous. She might reject my suggestion and huff off with her camera and her portion of the crew (most of them) and then what will I have? What I've just started will have to remain here, frozen in time — a story, like most, that never gets off the ground because it is little more than a lazy kite in a shed.

'Listen,' she says, and begins to read from a book she has just pulled out of her bag. I crane my head down to see the title. *More House*. I think for a moment, because the name means something more to me than the teacher you had in primary school who had white wispy hair, but nothing comes to mind.

'In 1814 in a house called More House, worked a girl called

the girl, who was rare because she had the power to transcend her lot.' The director clears her throat. Then continues: 'She gave birth to a son who was also rare because he stood up, out of time, in order to carry his mother's story to future generations, where her shame and her coldness could be stroked away gently by lack of detail. If this were a chess game, the girl would be the king and her son, Joey, would be the queen. He gets around. The space is temporal. The dimensions are pure quackery. But that doesn't make sense and so we'll ignore it and stick in a traditional description: *Her eyelashes were silver littered with silver glitter and her teeth chattered when the nights were cold.*'

The writer is me. I know her. She's been toying with these ideas, these people, for years now, rolling them around in her head, making shapes.

The girl that she's talking about blossomed one spring inside a diary that has since been burned at the stake. Her charred insignificance still enriches the soil of the Midwestern family that I used to nanny for, but its windows continue to spit words that I like — straight out at the immaculacy of golf.

Burning my diary never stopped me from writing. Those Midwesterners would've had to burn me to get results, which they didn't do — for fear I'd sue them.

The director turns a few pages, skipping ahead for something that will suit both of us, and then continues to read in her reading aloud voice: "Frank and Carol were my employers' names." [Sweet Jesus, this is my book!] 'And I speak to them and say, "Here is her resurrection. Here is the slick of her fiction running down my thigh. For you. Just for you. It catches your local priest by his skirt and says, Show me yours and I'll show you mine. I rub onions on your beady blue eyeballs and smile when I see the girl coming out of the pages that you set on fire. To disturb you, I get makeup to beat an egg-white and put some on her chin. It glistens there."

"I swallow. Every time," she says. "This is just a little that slipped out," taking it on her finger and sucking it off. Cold. Less tasty.'

'Hmm,' I say. I have been listening intently, except for a few points where my mind wandered off into *things to do* territory. Re-number the next chapter. Delete all chapters related to Frank and Carol (they are the seed but not the flower). Tell everyone that my writer's fog has lifted.

'There's something in there for both of us, no?' I say. 'A little love, a little evil.'

The director smiles. We may be onto something here.

# 5

The narrative sits at the hinge between 1814 and 2009. Two worlds rushing to greet each other from two different centur ies. The past laps at the present which becomes the past now and now and now and by the time you reach the end of the sentence it becomes ancient history, which is good for writers because it makes it more difficult for readers to detect errors. The odd historian coughs up his toast in disgust, but the rest of us say, 'Wow!' and 'Anything is possible.' Like the location of Joey's house, conveniently built on the original grounds of More House, which used to belong to my granny — before I killed her off and stole it for this novel. All mine.

I jot down the connections between Joey's house and More House under the heading *Coincidences*:

1. The ghost of the demolished house wears a white fog gown through which we see a row of brick housing.

2. The lawn that once swallowed a lady's bracelet now discreetly coughs it up into the digging fingers of a child. (Joey, age six).

3. Miners and their families live on what was once the Lord's acreage and have red bricks for backs.

4. A back lane where a carriage once deposited rich, flabby detritus now gives us the sound of fucking cats or cats fucking.

5. The la de da of a lawn party has been eclipsed by some D.H. Lawrence cock in the parlour.

6. And, of course, net curtains, which smother women no matter what class they're from, hang themselves suspiciously.

Her real hair colour nags bitchily at her sweet Marilyn blonde. Nostalgia is a sagging bore, but we have to begin somewhere. So why not at the roots that embarrass us?

Upon rifling through my granny's box of buttons I find one that I like. It once graced the coat of a girl who worked at More House. The button represents a seed that contains a tree that will grow so large it will need to be chopped down. Quickly, I don green tights and a pointy hat, and borrow an axe from a dad. But first I put the button into my mouth and listen to it scrabble along my teeth.

I don't know what she looked like or how old she was when it happened — or even what happened. I don't even know her name. She belongs to a brief one-line story I picked up from a button. The story grows in me. That's all. The one line is a fabrication that needs dressing and I dress it like a girl.

The story involves the relationship between the woman and her employer, a poet and Lord, who was her lover when I'm in one mood and her rapist when I'm in another. I know that a baby was born. What happened before and what happened after was too complicated to be written down on a button. This fabrication begins the moment I decide to take her baby, his bastard, to the edge of the family circle and put him down in the damp evening grass, beside a caterpillar. A moment that never comes.

This particular poet, I have decided, impregnated a significant number of his employees, but I have met only one so far — in the back lane behind the plural houses where all meetings take place. She did her best to provide me with details, but being between both scenes, as an actor, and chores, as a character, it wasn't like she had time to really spread the map out.

This is not a story about the injustices wrought upon women who find themselves in the shuttered houses of the rich.

Actually, this is not even a story.

# 6

I was born without a penis. My two brothers were born with them. My two sisters are the same as me and don't have penises either. So, that's two of us with penises and three of us without. I learned to divide a room up into groups — those with penises and those without — at an early age. My sense of smell helped me with this. The adult ones without penises usually had perfume on their faces or around their necks. Garlands of it. While the ones with tended to smell of hands that had come in from the garden and were yet to be washed.

The ones with penises mingled in the flowering haven of my mother's neck. She took down notes on everything they said. In shorthand. Like a secretary. And every evening she read over her notes before going to bed — her glasses, a bird perched at the end of nose, over whose wings she said goodnight.

Carving out boys was my mother's occupation. She carved them out of soapstone, out of wood, out of men. She even tried to carve them out of us girls. And oh, did we want to be carved! I stopped doing cartwheels and wore only trousers and hung out with shirtless men in the garden, in hope that I'd grow my own little hanging pepper — hanging down the vine of my thigh, hanging down with its veins and piss that could come out in a perfect arc onto the shed wall.

---

I met you, Stepfather, as I promised I would. In a hotel bar in the wood of the table and the way you fingered the pack of cigarettes etc. left a wick for this memory to burn. The beer light broke my heart and your concentration. One meeting was enough. And then you died. That was your logic, not mine. *Died* is my word, not yours. Roughly translated it means 'started a new family. Elsewhere.' I pretended that I was your wife and that we were going through a divorce. We sort of were, weren't we? And I thought about the time we drove to the airport in Vancouver and flew to California looking down at the neat land and wishing and how when we got to Los Angeles and a passenger on the bus asked if I was your girlfriend you winked at him, which meant 'yes,' and I immediately made the bus driver stop the bus so we could get off and you could buy me an ice cream, lickety-split Lolita in my knickers. It's awkward, that last sentence, to reflect its content.

It was you who raised this novel. You played your part and then you left, leaving me the gift of this wild and famished animal that is writing. I fed it and feed it and will continue to feed it. When I feed it, it smiles at me with bloodied bits of fat and gristle hanging from its teeth. I don't mind the horror. I always smile back. Sometimes the animal and I get separated. Between us a troop of distractions hover and shuffle and shift and we find ourselves alone in different rooms of the house you made me in. These are my worst times.

The house is a start. It'll do. Let's appraise the items carefully: the finger guillotine that somebody would later bring home from woodwork class, the pink vomit, the Hans Christian Andersen windowsill, the daddy less his long legs.

I gallop around the house, a horse on a mission to find a gap in the fence of my fate, but get nowhere on my two legs, my two small legs in their woollen tights. It is a winter house. Cold everywhere, except under my mother's Indian sheet where her warm breath meditates over the possibility that the world might actually be a colourful place. I graze the silent carpet close by, waiting for her to speak, fearful that the draught will change direction and turn her permanently mute.

You came at me with your army of vile fantasies, caught my sister by the hair and scalped her. You put me in a house and you rubbed away the windows and the doors, leaving only the chimney for my grandfather's pipe smoke to billow sadly out, up and away. You closed the curtains and made me play make-believe father and daughter games. I batted my eyelashes until they fell off. I hid my imagination inside my little white socks and buried them in the garden — one for this life, the other for the next. You set bees on me. You dug earth out of my tummy. You grated your voice at my door, letting it drip in the direction of the grain. Never against the grain. The world loved to shake your hand and give you its children to shepherd and everyone said things like 'He's so good with children!' while I stood there in my new body — I was barely four years old — holding on to your leg.

I stayed close to you because I was a clever ninny. I bandaged up the word *house* and wrote Home Sweet Home on it. Then I hung it up in the kitchen where it could soak up the smells of your Sri Lankan childhood. Icing on maggots. Cherries on rot. The word irony came later, in high school, along with the beds and backseats of zit-encrusted high-school boys. My makeshift heroes.

---

My mother falls in with the marmalade on my toast. Around the room objects are turning into words with definitions. My stepfather takes out a pencil and draws a clock on the wall. It speaks a language I have yet to learn. Time is my mother's weapon of choice. She takes it and measures herself a deep, gasping draft of it. Then she goes outside the drawing of our house with a suitcase, shouting over her shoulder that she isn't coming back. My older brother, folded up inside her suitcase like a teddy, because it is safer for him there than it is at home, is light enough to carry. She stays out long enough for four wasps to die in the honey water. Forever I am waiting for her, listening to the sound of my mouth chewing.

# 7

I have a dead woman to deal with. She's just a one-liner, like the rest of them. A button story. I want to know where she's from, this TV lady, bagged up and begging. Cast as Caucasian, just for the drama of her skin when they pull her from a river thanks to a tip from somebody's never-hurt-a-fly relative.

She gives her body up for inspection. Such generous plundering. Just look and she can be found in a state of decomposition in your very own neighbourhood. She is the local hero. Silent. Extraordinarily patient as they move her from one bag or metal bench to another or while a couple of sexy detectives flirt across her blue-grey breasts.

I know her from a time before TV. Hidden somewhere in the fields or woods around my friend Helen's house. She arrives in pieces, divided between various plastic carrier bags and the season is always autumn in the UK and fall in North America.

---

It is getting dark and we shouldn't be so far from Helen's house. A group of frightening men and their frightful girlfriends have left behind the ash pit of a fire, empty lager cans, fag butts. They have dragged a mattress from somewhere. Helen tells me what they've been up to. A dead sparrow on its back with its feet pronged and scratchy is what she labels and bags as evidence. Dead animals are always evidence. I do not want to be in the woods because it is to these woods that murderers go. Murderers and guys in leather jackets with their drunk girlfriends stumbling along beside them in shit-caked heels.

There is a bridge over a thin river. It holds many stories. The bridge separates the woods from the fields and a map somewhere just out of my reach attests to this. Helen's dog is up ahead snouting through tall grass. He will trot over the indents of pinned girls whose grass-flecked cheeks have been taken to the next world to be washed. He will sniff at a beetle, run at a living sparrow.

Whenever a piece of evidence shows up in the woods it unnerves me. It is getting darker and I know that by the time we reach Helen's back gate it will be night. Her mum will be angry, to mask her horror at having just seen a missing child 'show up' on the six o'clock news, but Helen will lip her back young lady and we will giggle and play piano while we wait for our tea: chips and beans.

The bridge is old and wobbly. A grandmother. 'It will fall soon,' Helen predicts. She jumps hard and I secretly hope she crashes through the bridge into the river below. She wouldn't be hurt. Ben would bark, because he barks at everything, and Helen and I would laugh. It would break the tension caused by the creeping, muttering darkness. She jumps again — harder — but nothing happens. 'I give this bridge one month,' she says. I wish she would stop messing around.

I wanted to find a dead body. That's why Joey finds one. All kids want to. They fantasize about coming across a bloated, naked body, half in the lake and half on the shore. It would be a thrill to be the one to tell. I was always on the lookout for dead bodies. Beaches were good places to look. There might be a corpse, or part of one, washed up on the sand or found wedged between some rocks after the tide had gone out. The closest I ever came to finding anything dead was the time I found a plastic bag half full of pigs' trotters. I opened the bag because I thought it would contain evidence, and it did.

There has already been a murder in this novel. The shoe is the most important piece of evidence and the only thing Joey will remember.

# 8

Casting have me sitting down on a stool in the garden. My back hurts. I feel squirmy, in danger. They want to know who's going to play Helen and why I've called her Helen and approximately how old she is. I tell them not to worry because Helen will just be herself, exactly as she is inside my imagination and that any tags hanging off details will get tucked in just before the camera rolls and no-one will know how or why she came into this story.

'They need more to go on,' says the director. 'They haven't even graduated from film school yet.'

'Just give her the kind of glasses kids wore in the eighties. Thick glass, pink rims (for girls), big lenses. She was funny as fuck, too. The kind of friend who makes you wet your knickers every time you see her.'

'And? Anything else?'

'She liked horror movies. A lack of imagination, I suppose. And she liked to be scared. It gave her immense pleasure to feel terrified and even more pleasure to terrify me. If she could have found the dead woman it would have been the highlight of her life. She would have taken one of her mother's high-heeled shoes, tocked off the heel and stuck it onto the side of her head. Then she would have turned into a zombie and chased me around the house, while her mother shouted, *Pack it in you two!!*'

The director turns to the woman in charge of casting and says, 'The girl can play her. Just give her some nerdy specs.'

# 9

The girl came out of my keyboard (how modern I am!) as late as 1999. Joey arrived much earlier. He started out with the kind of nasty streak that makes social workers nervous and he spent most of his time reading comics and birthing superheroes through Plasticine birth canals. Just to dismantle them. A slight tinge of obsessive-compulsive disorder allowed him to keep only green with green and blue with blue and red with red. That horrible green! Afterwards, he would fill the kitchen sink with hot water and dish soap and gently caress away the Plasticine deposits that had stuck to his mother's rolling pin. In fact, it was his parents' rolling pin and had actually never been used for anything *but* Plasticine, but Joey had a tendency, like the rest of us, and that means me, to stereotype all mothers as housewives. Well they are, aren't they? Exclamation mark. Look at my sisters and me in the kitchen making dinner for random boyfriends. There's the occasional 'chef' but he always needs special ingredients and a round of applause when he serves the food.

Housewife. Brick-and-mortar demolishing her market value. Joey's mother is, in fact, the composite of all my ex-boyfriends' mothers and the woman I am now beginning to think I may one day become. So meddlesome. So picky. So rifling through her son's drawers.

Joey hates her most of the time, mostly for marrying Mr. Nobody, but hate is a strong word, and such a mother would say something along those lines if you used it. Hate is pure and total. There is no swaying the mind of the hater. It is an unwavering spark of emotion. The sound of a burning match hitting water.

He is a nasty piece of work, lifting the dripping rolling pin from the water and running his hand back and forth along the wooden shaft. I'll have him meet a policeman in a back lane — the place policemen live — who will ask Joey what he has behind his back. 'Nothing much, just a rolling pin,' only he won't say anything of the sort because there is no reason to take it outside. His mother, as stereotype and I dictate, is always inside the house.

Joey, though, can usually be found sitting on the curb of a deserted street. Either that or he is behind the plural houses in the back lane. 'Ease in the back lane.' There is nothing on Joey's street. It is an empty stage. I have been too preoccupied with him to think up any secondary characters. The eye travels from the upstairs bathroom, where Joey's mother is distractedly sucking Mr. Nobody off (why did I have to write that?), to the curb directly below the bathroom window, where Joey is reading a *Batman* comic. (Some details are more important than others. Some brackets, too.)

If he tries to walk down the street, in either direction, he will meet the edge of oblivion in the form of a white field. Not snow, no, something less decadent. He will come face-to-face with the confines of his own head — where all good universes must come to an end in the end.

I must think beyond the confines of scenes, of moments. Bring in the cartographer! This *X* marks the spot where Joey saw the essential-for-a-first-novel dead woman. He was shocked mainly by how fake she looked and by her cliché hurray! white stilettos.

In my hand I have a black-and-white aerial shot of Joey sitting on the curb. His mother — free now — cranes from the upstairs window, her call caught in the grain of the photograph. But Joey's spine is curved right into the centre of the story on the tip of Aubrey Beardsley's fine tipped tool, away from his mother. Always.

If I put a pair of roller skates on Joey, he would roll first in one direction, stop, and then roll in the other direction. Then he would give the first direction another try. At that point he would look up at the sky, where I am, and for a moment would imagine that he could see me. And then, as if he had forgotten what he was supposed to be doing, he would sit back down and resume reading his comic.

There are no other children on this street, because there are no houses for them to live in. There is no grass — just a lot of dust and the brick house behind Joey that his mother is protruding from. If he walks through the house, though, and into the brick yard and through the high back gate he will be in a novel set in Yorkshire and written by somebody else. There will be plenty of children to play with, and women with fat arms pegging out washing, and a rough-looking boy with dirt-smeared cheeks building a go-cart with his dad.

There is always more than one possible life.

# 10

The girl is making trouble. It's a work day at More House so of course she has been given orders, but she is executing them huffily, hardly — like she thinks someone else should be doing them. I hand her a piece of paper that reads, *There was once a girl who was sent to work for a rich lord.* 'Ah!' she says, smiling. Thank God.

'And . . . ACTION!'

Her father walks beside her. She is not happy to have to be escorted through her days like a child (make sure she frowns here), but she is nothing more than a girl and needs help keeping her chin firmly pointed forward at a man (and has her chin up here). The road to the Lord's house is wet from a recent shower, and in the bright sunlight it makes sense that life is also described as a road. Progress is so pretty. It lightens the heart.

The father sees his daughter's future unravel its pulpy tongue and splash down onto the wet road. It is so exciting, he thinks, that he cannot help but grin. She will bring in a fine bushel of opportunity for mother to peel and pare. She will turn horseshoes on their heels.

The father and daughter don't speak. Emotion would rattle their words if they dared. "The Little Woman and the Proud Old Man" is the name of their fairy tale. It leaves little room for doubt. One stays behind in the cottage, while the other fucks and decorates a prince. One hears a bird in the forest singing the most beautiful song, while the other gives birth to an animal.

It is the blood of a wealthy bloodline that he thirsts for and so he offers his daughter's womb as a cup to be filled. The Lord has been rumoured to drink the blood of virgins, but virgins, reckons the father, have plenty to spare. 'Let him drink deep, my child. Raise us out of the coal. Be a cup and be filled. Or, if his lordship prefers, emptied.'

The girl remembers for a moment that her father is still walking beside her. She knows he will feel better if he presents her at the Lord's house. That's what other fathers in the village have done with their girls. How many have come out to live straight lives? How many have come out spoilt goods, old maids? The girl has already decided that this will not be her fate.

## 11

The Lord is an aggressive, moody man. He takes long strides and has a deep voice. If it is windy his hair is long enough to flutter bamboo about his hatless head.

'Where did you get him from?' I ask the director.

'From a 19th-century porn magazine. I tore him out for you. He's brooding and dark and he looks like he's been shagging all day.'

'He probably has. He'd better be able to get it up.'

He is heard, but not seen, an insomniac with a permanent hangover, purple under the eyes most of the time, demanding eccentric things at ungodly hours and obsessed with his own bowel movements. His day is divided into periods of work and pleasure. For every finished poem, a blowjob; for every completed review, a five-course meal; for every letter to a sexy cousin, a *ménage à trois*.

The Lord doesn't employ the girl — Hannah does. Hannah is the cook, according to me. She is fat and loving and she takes good care of her girls. Her husband is a miner who has a talent for impersonation. He is able to pull the Lord off better than the Lord himself. After a particularly stressful week at work Hannah comes home and gets her husband to 'do the Lord' until it hurts her sides.

The girl shares a room with Hannah for the first few weeks at More House because the butler, Steven with a *v*, needs his truant son to help him carry a bed up to the maids' quarters. And don't get any ideas, because from this vantage point, perched like a bird on the gate to my imagination, nobody stays awake long after the candles are put out with spit-licked fingers.

'Psst! Grace.'

Sleep is arrived at with a feeling of blissful exhaustion — a feeling reserved for the hardworking people of this world, of any time period.

Solomon is the name of the truant son. Steven and Solomon are both male names that begin with S. S is the first letter in the word sex. Sex is always, always on its tip toes looking in. Marginalia. She wore marginalia in her hair and it smelled like heaven.

Everything is falling apart. Good.

# 12

The trees bend and kiss me. Both Joey and the girl are sleeping, root-twisted like sibling cats. The trees bend and kiss them too. There is guilt, but there is also relief and the common sense to escape without asking them whether or not they want to escape too. Do it alone. It's less hassle.

Anyway, the only option is to do it alone. The trees have gone out of their way to greet me, but I do not owe them anything. I let them worry over me for a while before pushing their frilly greens away. The breeze can listen. In their sleep both characters can hear. They are never for a moment unconscious of my existence. They do not need the things that the rest of us need. I put them to bed unnecessarily, because they do not need sleep. They do not do anything. It is painful to imagine what they would look like if they came to life. One moment one way, the next moment another; parts missing because I haven't bothered to imagine them. Would it matter if I described them both to you now? Would the colour of their hair or skin or eyes bring them to life? I do not know enough about anatomy to know where to put this kidney. It's hot with blood. Shall I bother with an appendix when it will probably end up getting removed? I want to make something out of 'there was a boy' and 'there was a girl.' The only thing we know is that the boy is not a horse and the girl is not a tiger. Nor is the boy a tiger or the girl a horse. They are on their knees pleading for adjectives and lungs. I have never written a novel before and do not know the protocol.

'Where are you going?' asks the director.

'For a walk in the cool green woods,' I say.

'Shall I walk behind you with the camera to catch your moving hams?'

'No. Focus on your own hams.'

'I don't have any. You haven't imagined me yet.'

She looks sad. Far away.

'I can see you perfectly,' I say. 'It's like looking into a mirror.'

Description gets spread out over the filmed body. You see the hoop earrings or the silk scarf, or you don't. Joey is working for me, but I don't know what he looks like. He's vague. A teenage boy at a train station. My cousin James. The lankiest legs this side of. Connor's hair. My brothers. He must be Caucasian because I am. Isn't that a shame? There are boys in India. There are boys strolling the streets of South Korea. He's barely in focus and always behind a shimmer of heat or pushed by a windstorm wearing a Dustin Hoffman jacket. Riding a bike with no hands is so 1980s, but that's the look I'm going for here. And Jamaica.

It's the same story with the girl. She might have dark brown hair. Actually, I'm quite sure that she does. She wears it back, off her face, despite the fact she doesn't have a face. She certainly has hands. She is a Yorkshire lass and, like my grandmother Dora, a Jew by rumour only.

I am their mother and agent, at the verge of everything, at the cracks and fissures, squashing their dreams under the weight of my own un-lived ones. I push them onto the audition stage in their tight new shoes and order them to tap dance for the nice man.

The truth is they hate me — unless I am telling a story with them in it. My leaving tonight is not a big deal. The woods let me enter and then they let me set up camp. When I feel lonesome I put my arms around the trunk of one of the trees and squeeze. Nobody comes looking for me, and things go on as they always have. Behind closed doors.

# 13

The girl walks down an empty country lane. Behind her are More House and the house where I keep the Brontë siblings with their wet skirts and trouser hems. Behind her is the church that I've never seen anybody go into or come out of, but that makes More a hamlet. In the field to her left, cows are forecasting rain; in the cottage garden to her right, lupins are bringing out their finest pink china; and to either side, the hedgerow is guarded by lines of cowslip — a tall and intellectual flower.

She is not the movie star we might have expected, with her stiff frock and disappointingly flat chest. Note to wardrobe: a little here, a little there. We have seen such flattery before: girls arriving at school dances, removing long coats to reveal their mother's dresses — gaping slightly under the arms to the beginnings of secondary sex characteristics made out of toilet paper.

Hannah has sent the girl to the village shop with a list. The walk between the house and the village is always pleasurable, because for the duration of the walk the girl is free. But for the writer, there isn't much to go with. It is boring to describe the girl walking for an entire hour, unless you get behind her and watch her moving hams bloom or unless she meets a talkative wolf in sharp duds who has a long, slavery slab of a tongue and a little red dick poking out of its hairy Jack Russell case. Which happens.

Yes, a girl in nature must be met and seen, must be pinned to a hedge by the force of some distant relative's horse breath;

must be seen by wolf-whistling farmers leaning on spades; must be caught in a storm that leads her to seek shelter in an old shack where somebody long lost or WANTED raps on the door and brings the rain in with him.

There must be a broken ankle and a peddler; a sty to cross and a bearded man with wet, pædophile eyes; bluebells to kiss the dew-soaked trouser hems of a romantic Londoner; and berry-stained fingers that he puts into his mouth and sucks the invisible cum out of. And loosening hair. Running from him and tripping over into love, into puddles. Letting go of all pretence as he introduces his manhood to your nether regions. And later, stained petticoats scrunched up at the bottom of a washing basket to be mused over by the meddlesome fingers of a housewife.

---

When the girl returns from the village, the Lord looks up from his writing desk and sees her emerge from the hem of her shortcut out into the grassy meadow, mowing a trail with her skirts. The huff of a budding storm brings her forward over the ground like a cross father (I've imported all of the above details from a box marked *Merchant Ivory*).

That evening, in the warmth of the Lord's bedroom, she must act like she is having a fucking good time before she tells him that she has no dowry. A tree falls in the woods, shattering a nest of eggs over a wet bush.

# 14

This paragraph is a painting that you will one day see in an art gallery. It is one, simple scene: A girl in a blue dress sits on a railway platform with her legs dangling over the tracks into a slow river. A water boatman skims by, ferrying the roe of some mourning sticklebacks over to the other side. And, yes, he walks on water, miraculously.

A train is coming in the painting. It is panting.

---

I hate girls and it makes me want to fuck them is the thought that is crossing my mind as I cross the courtyard, designed by Arthur Erickson, and see a water boatman on the surface of the pond that takes me to another light gentleman — on mill-weed in Sandwich and close to my searching net, almost willing. He is a slightly miraculous prophet, I would say, but I am nearing thirty-five, the bus loop and apathy, so I'm not going to open that can of spiritual worms. Not yet.

I used to get my best friends to make out with me, until the cookery teacher — Mrs. Schuster, circa 1954 — outed me in earshot of the entire class.

'So, I hear you're a lesbian.'

'No. What's that?'

I have here her ten identical sinks and the smell of butter on white skin; her talcum-powdered mole against greaseproof paper; margarine on our little-kid fingers slipping over the grease the tin. Did you grease the tin? Things slide out when you do.

I wish I could bring my own wooden spoon from home. It would smell of my family. Mrs. Schuster touches my spoon at the handle, showing me how to stir things without splattering them over the floor. I do anyway, with my jerky elbow bones and I shall clean it up young lady as she swings round upon a deliciously sweet and clean tooth-picked cake. Oh, that's very good, you beaming, toothy horse-child. Mrs. Schuster sticks her tongue into the beaming girl's mouth and wiggles it around, probing for bits of shredded coconut, angelica, candied fruit. They have their margarine hands all over each other's white, puffy faces. The girl is turning into an apron. Help her!

Mrs. Schuster's liver-spotted hands open out our fists and turn them over, looking for dirt. She sniffs our fingers greedily, because she loves the smell of little girls cooking with animal fat. She loves the sugared taint of our sin on our skin. Lickable moles.

My butterfly cakes have wings that are so fat they look like wide slugs. There are hundreds and thousands under my fingernails. I look at my reflection in the pregnant belly of a dessert spoon and wonder why I was born.

The slow river is cool and coated in mill-weed. My net cuts a black path through the green, dragging, dragging, closing after. A water boatman skims by. Another. Two more.

The river is anything but sugary. It is home to the contents of my fishing net. The trailing sex of creatures hangs its infection over the bamboo edge of the net, attracting mites and skimmers. I lay the net down in the grass and open my remember-to-bring biscuit tin. My butterfly cakes, lighter and fluffier than Mrs. Schuster wanted me to believe, flicker a moment, rise up through insect traffic, then plunge — miniature sponge eagles into the river.

Once the last cake has flown the tin I scatter the stray hundreds and thousands at the bulrushes and go straight home, straight.

# 15

Late evening. The grounds of More House. A pond with trash in it: a milk jug, blossoms, the crumbs of scones, a Cadbury's Fruit and Nut wrapper. Two actors, a man and a woman, sit on a bench in a pool of generator generated light waiting to be called back on set. The man takes a stolen beer from his backpack and passes it, tss, to the woman, and then he takes one for himself. The woman is finding it hard to get comfortable. She fidgets, sometimes putting her legs over the man's lap. She rubs his head. Scratches it. They discuss what it feels like to have a good art moment and what it feels like between such moments, when it seems like there is no hope of another. He calls them 'moments of grace' and says that faith is both necessary and practical and then he opens a second beer:

*Man* So, you're writing a novel.
*Woman* Something like that.
*Man* Can I read it?
*Woman* When it's finished. You won't like it. It's weird.
*Man* We'll see.
*Woman* Yeah, we'll see (laughs).
*Man* Are you going to tell me the truth?
*Woman* No, I don't like the truth.
*Man* But the truth is essential.
*Woman* For some people, perhaps, but not for me.
*Man* Are you lying now?
*Woman* Yes, always.
*Man* I thought as much.

They are silent for a while.

*Woman* Want to be in it?
*Man* What?
*Woman* The novel.
*Man* Sure.
*Woman* OK. Sit very still. Don't move a muscle.
*Man* OK.
*Woman* OK. I'm the short woman — think Emily Dickinson — and you're the man with the hat:

The pond swirls, at its centre a dark and sucking circle. A flock of rowing boats, painted various colours, enter the hole in miniature after being abandoned by a group of startled children. The udder of a cow, caressed by a milkmaid in an afternoon meadow, drips decadently. The stool has three legs and creaks under the weight of the milkmaid who is 60 percent soft pudding and 40 percent starched cotton. Walkers with canes and parasols and pet monkeys made of various coloured dots spot the scene. The passengers on a train lean from the windows with their arms waving at people on the platform whose arms are also waving. (Yes, this is the image that sticks when I throw it at the wall.) All except one. A rather petite woman who stands at the far end of the platform (the camera is wherever you happen to be) with her arms akimbo (because there always has to be someone). (Are we sinking? Are we sinking?) It is a good riddance disguised as a farewell. She has crossed paths too often with fickle lovers who don't dare even glance out of train windows for fear of changing their minds. He fussed over his food too — and she hated that. Tss!

A man sits on the platform bench with his hat pulled over his eyes and his shoulders slumped forward out of the line of narrative. He will not look at the petite woman, even when she passes and the hem of her skirt brushes his recently polished shoes. He looks at her hem, though, remembering that blanket of a saying, 'There are other fish in the sea,' and look!

there they are, swimming about here and there across the on-set station. He pulls back his shoulders, tips his hat away from his eyes, and looks at the woman as she crosses the path of a child carrying a bright fat balloon. The child is wearing a blue dress, or blue pants if he is a boy, and has the softest hair.

Let's say the child is the water-coloured girl who is about to get crushed by a slow-moving train. The art gallery that exhibits the painting is yet to exist, but on opening night someone will ask: 'Why doesn't she just get out of the way?' The answer to that question, caught only by the retina of the girl in the painting, makes its slow way upstream. The answer to why the stream meanders to the left and right of the narrative has something to do with an ox-bow lake. From the sky we shall call it a snaking waterway. Note the way that the land pulls on the water and the water wears down the land.

The woman exits the platform through a gate to the left of the stationhouse. Which is Sunday. The man follows her and catches her with gentle fingers. He knows, because he has read the script, that she is relieved to be rid of her fussy lover and he is eager to offer himself as a replacement.

'Your shoes need re-heeling,' he says, aiming his camera-eyes at Emily's heaving breasts, which are so large it seems she might topple over from their weight at any moment.

'How would you know?'

'I'm a shoemaker.'

She lifts her skirts and looks down at her shoes, turning first one shoe and then the other in order to inspect each heel. She can see what he means.

'Let's go back to my shop,' he says.

She brushes away his pickup line, like a leaf from a coat, but then thinks better of it, picks it up and pops it into her mouth. It tastes of carrots. She can already feel her belly warming and turning colours. She tells him to take her to his shop immediately; to his dark, back bedroom; to his single bed.

'All the better to keep you next to me,' he wolves in her ear, making sure to leave a little spittle behind. For the air.

'Take me there!' she says, horrified by the urgency in her

voice — an urgency that wouldn't be there if this weren't a porn movie hell-bent on getting gratuitous narrative out of the way to make room for pussy and cock.

—

Now there is a rather long silence. The actor is considering his new role. Sexually satisfied. A little tipsy. Warm in the spotlight that has spread the urgency of her lovemaking evenly over his skin. Beer in the centre radiating out.

'I'm a replacement lover only?' asks the man.

'I suppose so.'

'I'd prefer a more substantial role.'

'You are more important than it seems. Without you, the murder couldn't happen.'

'I'm a murderer?' He looks gleeful, excited, like Helen did when she was scaring me.

'I haven't decided yet, but probably not. You're the maker of the murder weapon though.'

'Which is?'

'A shoe.'

'A shoe?!'

'With very sharp heels.'

'Oh,' he says, trying to do the math.

'In the end it won't make any difference whether you're a shoemaker or not. You just need to have a decent job. Women like that. It makes them horny and that'll make the scene more realistic.'

# 16

When a baby is born at More House he or she or she-he or he-she is taken away. Immediately. Hannah keeps the system running smoothly, not because she is in any way supportive of the Lord's behaviour, but because she knows that preventing contact between the mother and child lessens the pain of the theft.

The girl is too weak from labour to protest. After her baby has gone the room gets really quiet, huddles down into its quietness and tries to beckon the girl into it. But when the curtains join in and try to kiss the room dark, she thinks, 'No, not now,' prompting the writer to send in the brightest godlight we have ever seen. A line, a slit, a margin down her sinking, emptied belly, down between her tired legs, over the oak-fern carvings, along the floor, followed by a beetle and a mouse back to its source and then out.

It is a rich man's bed, a rich man's room, and the girl is trying to focus on the expensive decor that she plans to one day redo to her own tastes. But it isn't helping. She is of two halves and minds. Split one for the practical outcome, the other for the loving animal push of her labour. Does she take on the baby or does she take on the man?

That same morning — it is a Monday — Hannah takes the baby to the orphanage in the basket of her bicycle. He reaches the vicar's house by Friday, wrapped in brown paper and tied up with string. The string is cut and he is christened Joseph.

Clearly it is Monday's child who is full of woe. For four nights he sleeps with other babies in a room with no mobiles.

Heads peer into his cot. Women pass, clicking — their hen breasts heaving, their sagging faces flushed with blood from leaning in to inspect other women's produce. On Friday morning one type of crying (loneliness) is replaced by another (sadness). Loneliness is when there is nothing to be sad about — at least you have you. Sadness is when the light fades faster than you thought it would or when the lights come on and you are caught.

The net that catches Joey is the kind that children buy from shops in seaside towns. It takes less than a week for the netting to tear from its bamboo frame — it is thin, young bamboo.

---

The girl needs an escape route — a tunnel, a secret passage and some sobering plans. More House is a maze of doors and mirrors and windows and mirrors again. Keeping. Stay with me. The house is an embrace that can periodically be tender. A Brontë storm framed by every window in the house is mocked by beds that are layered so high that the sleeper is almost winded upon climbing into bed. A material reality. Getting out of bed and getting into it. Knocking on the door of a house and then being let in. Being let out two hours later and walked by an umbrella-carrying butler to an awaiting carriage.

It has rained every day this week. It has rained on the girl and her son. And their masters are both riding through it — one from the tavern, the other to the church — while work is being done by girls and wives in houses for miles around.

The dripping Lord enters the house booming orders that scatter workers in a myriad of directions, all of which pass a mirror. The windows are ordered shut, the fires stoked. A bath is ordered drawn and quartered an apple from the cellar that has not yet been walked on by beetles or mice. The girl scatters out with the other maids. We cannot focus as she spins from one room to the next, wearing the expected black and white uniform of one of our leggier fantasies. Lifting her skirt behind as she spins, she is a doll on the wind of his whiskied orders. A fantastic material reality. An embrace from behind. The camera traps her in the same manner that the Lord trapped her and made a son come out of her who passed from the midwife to the orphanage matron to the vicar's wife and eventually, on the day of his christening, to the vicar.

The Lord tends to call on his maids between the hours of 6 and 7 PM, before his five-course daily embrace with gluttony. It is the girl's turn today. She stands by the door with her hands under a pile of towels, so high that they almost cover her nose. He likes the veiled look, having spent time with his toes in the sand of Orientalism. The air in the bathroom is humid. The Lord is a steamed-up apparition.

'Come here.'

She soaps his skin. The dark hairs on his body, tendrils of seaweed, flicker to the fickle current of the water. He reclines with his eyes closed and his mouth open — his hands dangling one to either side of the bathtub. She washes his penis as if it were a carrot, because she has to, because the soup is coming to a boil.

Suddenly he squeezes a hand around hers, then grips the back of her neck where the hair is as soft as a muzzle and pushes her head forward over the rim of the tub. Sour water sloshes alongside his entering root vegetable, pushes past the rocky curve of her teeth.

Soon she is bobbing in time with a toy sailboat, her eyes nesting; the slapping lap of bathwater distracting her from the sound of her own sloppy mouth. The front of the girl's dress is wet. Two round patches. A little of the deep sloshing water must have slipped over the edge of the bathtub, or at least that's what it looks like.

Not stopping, bobbing at his nest dutifully, she shifts her eyes slightly to see the tombstones of both his feet poking from the grey landscape. A churchyard in winter. Her son's second father, the vicar, now hurrying past the graves of his flock to a wet horse.

The girl waits for the next sentence, pressing hard at the pain in her vagina, while the narrative drips undetected down her leg. There is meaning in her posture when she comes out of labour and realizes what is going on. Hannah has made a pathway from the birth to the window by dragging the bloody placenta along the floor. She crosses lines with her witchery, but harmless ones. It doesn't matter what has happened. It only matters what is yet to come.

The girl soon feels strong enough to get up and does. The wood of the floor feels like a firm solution to the passing cloud of her child's birth. The boy, for it was certainly a boy, got hoisted on the wings of inconvenience up and out of More House. The realization that he has gone grips her and hurls vomit from her mouth. There are words, too, but they come out reeking of acid, unable to exist for long in the cutting light of potential hope, because there is — there always is.

Love wells. Love rivers and shines.

I can see the way. It comes to me in Chinese characters. It comes to me under loud water. The girl's maternal instinct must be stronger than her material one. Duh.

'I want my baby,' whispers the girl. 'I want my son.'

'But that's not even an option,' says Hannah. 'Either historically or here in the fiction of this woman who is writing us up from the slag heap of servitude. So think of something else I could get for you — like a cold compress or a nice cup of tea, love.'

# 17

Fifteen years later on a Wednesday's child is loving and giving a coin to a butcher on London Road, the girl sees her son pass by. She knows it is him because she's read the script. She grabs her bicycle and follows him with her moving ham. A crow. The winter evening darkens the lane and the village and the surrounding fields. She is having trouble catching up to his lankiness until he trips, purposefully, plotfully, over the straying root of a tree. She leans her bike against the tree and extends her hand to him. Her fingers have never even touched him. 'Mum?' he says. The knee of one of his trouser legs is torn and wet. 'I will sew you together with my needle and thread,' she says. He takes her hand and brings it to life. Out of this book.

They ask me for a private space, a space to talk up the laughter of revenge. I give them Helen and I's mattress woods, on a slight incline of night, with cool, damp moss covered over by a blanket that Joey has brought with him from the vicar's house.

She wants to tell Joey who his father is, but how can she tell him that his father is a rutting stag? That he did her against the larder counter, then slunk away like a poisoned animal? Or a rough sketch. Or a steep incline. Or fucking. Or a parting of the legs. Or an oil painting. Or a tiger stalking. Or a field mouse on a stalk. Or the tiniest detail erased. There are no words coming.

How can she tell him that afterwards she sat on the floor for over an hour? It was cold, but she didn't notice. He slowly dripped out of her, drying to the skin on her inner thighs, which she picked and rubbed at absentmindedly, while somewhere in the house she pictured him finishing off his cheese sandwich and glass of wine. A pig-faced twat.

Candles were spit-fingered out or lights turned off, depending on the year. A window blackened. Then another. The warm kitchen waited for the girl to return to its story, but she knew that she would have to find a new plot to tie around her wrist — this time so it wouldn't be able to run away.

It wouldn't make sense to tell Joey the feelings of a mother afterwards. Either in the warm room or on the cold floor. The deep ore would now begin to wait to come to light.

'What have you got for me?' asks the director, while using her hands to indicate to Joey and the girl that she wants them to sit farther apart on the blanket.

I clear my throat and then begin reading from a piece of paper I have pulled out of my pocket and unfolded: 'This scene consists of a thin strip of land that backs onto woodland that is also fairly shallow. All I have is this strip of earth — some left-to-right, and right-to-left intention. A few twigs in her hair, a leaf in his, and a dirty thumbnail (Joey's). And, after, many nights spent alone staring out of windows. That melancholy space of the windowsill. Forehead numb from the cold pane. And much, much more. Like some DOLLY SHOTS, for example.'

When I finish reading and look up the scene is already on.

The girl takes a stitched leather penis from her bag and shows it to her son. 'I wanted you to see this,' she says. 'It's your father. I made it myself.'

## *Aside*

> *It is exactly the same shape as my stepfather's! The same map of veins. The same cool rage spreading over my belly and lower back like the movement of the Nazis across Europe, in red, in black. Is the same penis that stuck out at me, a hitchhiker's thumb at the edge of the highway trying to catch my ride. Come along then,*

*motherfucker, come along down this wide highway. We will stop for some aggressive fucking at a picnic area and you will show me your TA! DA! penis and I will sing* Glory, Glory, Hallelujah *and fashion it and make it fashionable and hang it between the legs of my main character and give her full rights to the blueprints of your map of veins and pubes.*

Joey takes the phallus from his mother's hand and turns it over.

'It's very big, isn't it?' As an actor, he wants to laugh — shake off the character he's been given with a loud explosion of laughter. So he does.

As an actor, the girl laughs too. And the director. And the entire cast and crew standing off set.

I am the only one not laughing.

'Stop it!' I shout. 'This is costing money. Just finish the scene.'

The girl looks down at her lines: 'Your father is made of leather and stuffed with sawdust, but you should still try to respect him, even if just a little.'

She carries her rapist's excuses in an embroidered handkerchief. She figures that if they are surrounded by pretty flowers they will be more easily accepted by her son, who she wants to be happy, so happy. The little pegs jar the back of her throat. *Las palabras* are foreign, mottled by the floor of a forest she has never visited, caught in the sickly sweetness of honey. She tries to rescue them, one by one, but by now they are dead wasps.

'Forgive me for letting you go, Joey,' she whispers, intending to say it more loudly.

'You mean, for putting your financial security, ego and revenge plot above my well-being?'

'I suppose so,' she says. 'It seems that way now. But at the time it was only a matter of being a young, naïve girl.'

'Sure, I . . . um . . . forgive you,' he replies, looking down at the script.

They are sitting on cold, temporary ground, on a set that has a woodland backdrop and a few leaves and twigs that have been casually dropped here and there. Behind them are painted deer that will never run away and birch trees imported from Bambi with bark that will never peel. Look behind you! There is nothing there and there never will be.

'It is proof of where you come from. You come from a dismal and absurd place. But I'm not the one writing the script.'

'Is that even in the script?' says Joey.

'Wasn't the penis thrown away years ago?' asks the director. 'I'm sure it . . .'

'STICK TO THE SCRIPT!' I shout.

Even though little more than a well-endowed porn actor trying to make his big break in real film, the Lord is outraged by the competition. Grudgingly, he puts his own penis into a drawer, tucking it away gently under a stack of nightshirts. For now he will sulk, but later he will get used to the idea of the girl shooting sawdust into his ass.

---

This is not happening. There is nothing. Pornography doesn't slay our little hearts. Except for the time the fly circled her bum in the orchard or the time he came all over her glasses and she looked sad, like she didn't know how she'd gotten herself into such a predicament. I'm not even sure how the girl cycled from More House in 1814 all the way down to London Road, Deal, Kent to buy ham from Helen's father. Or why there is a ham in the novel of a vegetarian being carried in the basket of a Jew. Or how Joey came all the way from 2009 on foot. A Thomas Hardy map might come in handy here.

# 18

The girl is wearing a T-shirt that says *Actress with a Migraine*. She is drinking tea prepared by one of the over-eager extras. 'The thinnest slice of cake, please.' Look how her lips tighten to imitate the anorexic slice.

The Lord, currently off work and not needed until tomorrow, is watching her from a dark corner of the studio. He has his hands in his deep, silk-lined pockets. She won't notice that look scraped from his plate to hers, or the dribble-stained silk, or the silt layer where his heart has been marooned. The top of the page is turning. She turns to the sound of a broom and Grace clicking slowly off set, also done for the night. All that is left is yesterday's backdrop — deer grazing eternally in a painted forest.

There's something on its way. A carriage? A baby? The Lord will be at the studio door holding an umbrella that she will decline. She's not bothered. He will follow her and he will rape her, but she's not bothered.

No one has ever been raped in a sentence. Nothing has ever happened on a page. It's as dry as a bone in here. Painted deer. Still mouths. It's a still life.

The girl revels for a moment in the silence, brushes cake crumbs from the corners of her mouth, picks up her handbag and leaves. Outside she is met by the Lord, in full costume. He steps into the light now spilling from the opened studio door, holding out a creepy umbrella, which she pushes away with a 'No, thank you.' He follows her anyway, holding the umbrella over her rush.

The top of the page is dog-eared. There is no one here. The church hall doesn't echo the tinny fingers of a piano. Come back tomorrow. The rest of the characters have either gone home or are sleeping in their trailers. I want to wake them but I have no plans, only the rough sketch of a map.

The narrative is on its way. Be patient. A taxi is waiting outside. Its driver has deep pockets. A voice and a face come tumbling in, tumbling after. He is leaking liquor fumes out of his mouth and up her nostrils. Later there is a rape. It happens in a sentence. He will say he loves her and then he will rape her in the letters *R*, *A*, *P* and *E*. No one has ever been raped on a page. The page is being turned by a large hand. Why is it frightening? Because it reminds her.

A film set miraculously descends. *The girl's trailer. The middle of the night. All is quiet.* There is something on its way, but she doesn't know what it is. Breakfast? The catering boy? These are the kind of ordinary things a person thinks about afterwards. The clock needs winding. There are leftovers in the fridge. Cake, she thinks. It's just a thought; just a very thin slice. Such things happen. At least she isn't dead.

# 19

The kitchen is an important location in this novel. It signifies the blah-de-blah of the blah-de-blah. In it, moist crumbs not yet separated from the body of a cake long to fall onto my granny's bosom, just so they can get brushed off onto the lawn, pecked up by a starling and then shat out from a high altitude onto the windshield of my parents' car. Wherever it is. Wherever their holiday has fallen upon them.

Afternoon tea is carried out to the garden on a tray by the eldest and most sensible child. Me. Granny leans back on her deckchair and pretends to have the afternoon in her lap. She dollops cream onto each of our plates, spoons strawberries, but not because she loves us. It is clear that spoiling our sweet teeth is part of a show she is putting on for our parents. After they have backed down her driveway, waving excitedly and making inaudible jokes about getting rid of us for two weeks, the curtains will drop and we will creak about More House while Granny and her husband methodically intoxicate themselves. Once the car has gone, the pinky-smeared plates will be stacked and taken into the kitchen by the child we shall call 'me'.

---

I stand at the kitchen sink looking out at nowhere in particular. My brothers and sisters have charged off to chase or be chased. They are in the beech copse, under the din of rooks. I am the poor daughter, inside, out of the cool thrill of play; pale and destined to become more so with my Little Polly Flinders-singed toes and my Little Match Girl burnt fingertips.

I stay in the kitchen long enough to feel abandoned; long enough to be there at the start of the next scene.

The girl sits beside the stove waiting for her hair to dry. She is alone in the kitchen. (Well, minus the director, the crew and me — now perched on the shoulders of some grizzly Californian man who, thinking I am an orphan, is practising for when he can adopt me.) The dishes have all been washed and dried and stacked in cupboards and drawers (by poor little me) and now it is a warm room. The only light comes from a candle beside the stove and that means mood. She pushes a needle with its thread tail through thin, brown leather and then she pulls it out a stitch. She continues sewing down one side and up the other until she has a long pocket to stuff. Which she does. With sawdust. Pushing it down with the handle of a wooden spoon to its fat and hard brim.

I take a photo of her. Later, at the wrap party, I surprise her with it. The picture stays with her for many years, transferred from one handbag to the next, because it makes her laugh. On the back she has written *Cock Maker.*

Where she got this idea from is anybody's guess, but it makes sense that she fashion herself after a man. She thinks that once her newly made penis is resting snugly against her pubic bone, she will be able to enter the drawing room undetected. Her sawdust and leather scent will put off even the most astute, pricked-eared misogynist. She will become invisible.

The girl makes sure that her penis is large without needing to place another order for leather. She fashions it after her dear father. To every small child, looking up at that sky with its one rain cloud of pubic hair, there is no other word for it: big.

Feeling her bath-damp hair between her fingers she looks behind her for the part she doesn't understand. But there is nobody there. No witnesses. She wants somebody to tell her to drop the spoon, to put away the notion that she can cross-dress her genitalia is such a beautiful word.

The girl holds her breath and her penis. 'I have no shame,' she decides, as she walks to the larder for tomorrow's vegetables and the next scene.

'And . . . ACTION!'

Striding along his hallway is the Lord, passing through slats of silver moonlight that bless a cat here, a hat stand there.

It is a small-*p* paradise that the Lord is in. The verb 'to stride' is wrong but I keep it because it is almost strict and almost pride. Let words go. They do not belong to you. Release them from their black wire cages, out into the corridors of your texts.

Get the light right. When is light really silver? '*His* hallway' is good. It is important to signal inheritance, possession, the fist that banks the counted and then re-counted bills. The material dream is forever a dirty surface made slippery by too much rubbing. It's impossible to get off if you think about it incessantly. Flapping, failing. Running desperately, with your fatty wheeze, but never taking off. It might not change, so focus on the here and now, on getting off quickly, bathed in silver, and for certain. Some dreams do cum.

The Lord enters his kitchen. Eat here. Cut there. Bleed there. Knife here. There kettle. There copper. A sliver of onion lost here.

Lighting technicians are getting fired by the day.

# 20

These are two scenes, folded in upon each other and made into one. A melancholy maid combing her wet hair before my granny's Aga, while unbeknownst to the camera, she fixes herself a penis. A ravenous Lord, hounding around the kitchens after a day out hunting, only to stumble across the first porn movie I ever saw. In Kelowna. Of a maid with floury hands and too many skirts.

The director is impressed with the economy of it all.

'Where are we?' she asks, rolling up her sleeves.

At this point the Lord is looking for food and the larder has her legs spread. Wet your index finger Dr. Who? Dog-ear the place that gets you off and then draw your student's attention to the top of page, whatever page it happens to be in this book. Begin reading aloud in your reading aloud voice. Focus on the curl of the line, up into the belly of the cow, the heifer, the bitch. The Lord is an instrument of gynæcological genius. His hat is overflowing with semen, so rich with sperm that its banks are crowded with fishermen. My ancestor was a fool to make something out of her plate of egg and sperm. If I wanted to, I could pick up the moment of conception and swaddle it to death. That would shut me up.

Why give Joey life? He is little more than lines of words. The girl too barely scrapes together an existence and wouldn't have been a story passed from one of my family members to the next if I hadn't been at the end of the telling — hands cupped, imagination turned up to maximum causing my head to shake so violently that none of her lines could settle.

She comes with her locket-portrait 1814 face, her son little more than a seed caught between teeth. Which is sometimes a big deal. Stuck. Brought along because there is nobody available to babysit him. Somebody has to tell the story, but first somebody has to care — hence the inclusion in this novel of the Lord, whose sperm, swimming across a Trivial Pursuit board in search of pie, is bent on providing lonely academics with an opportunity to blush proudly.

Stories are liquid and exist at a cellular level. They dribble and splutter; spit and run. I find a plot and press it between two glass slides. Under the microscope everything becomes clearer. I watch the girl's molecules breathe colour into and around Joey and the Lord. I see their blood pump away from their hearts to spray the arm of a river. Microscopic salmon jump desperate at my net. My white coat is stained with other books' experiments. The gall of a frog. The slick of a ribbon of kelp. The flippant rustle of dead horsetail. I wipe mill-weed off my hands, off my pond of a brain, off my darkening history of reading. I tug at the collective unconscious and it comes tumbling down to heap upon me.

---

He is looking for a thick slice of bread folded back towards itself in the hope of finding strong cheddar. And a glass of wine. Red, like a hood.

The larder is occupied. The girl is bent over a box of onions that shed themselves into her loving fingers. He stands in the door frame thinking he is quite possibly a masterpiece.

'Stop!' She freezes. It figures. He momentarily enjoys the vista of her back widening and shrinking. 'Get up.'

The girl stands and turns and places both her hands behind her on the larder counter. Beneath her the floor looks plain — like a floor does.

Turning, placing, rummaging, rustling. The verbs are moving and we are with them all the way. Take this scene and spin it. Call back the last lightning technician. We shouldn't have fired him. I think he's my dad and anyway it's too late to hire a new one. Place the candle in the path of a lady's busy fan. The bread and cheese cannot satisfy what is fattening and heightening and hardening in his trousers. Come on! Get on with it, exclamation mark! The hems are dry. The striding has been down a hallway, not through a meadow. There is no sound of a riding crop whacking the shit out of a rustling gang of August grass.

The seeds of this scene have now germinated. They want to sprout out of the soil; to build and brew. The verbs are moving. It's a long hallway. The Lord takes long strides. The light in the larder comes from a candle and casts shadow fingers over the food. He came for a snack, but is now thinking more along the lines of a feast.

The girl is breathing like girls do. Nothing special. The Lord is rising to greet the fabric of his trousers. The lighting is perfect. Keep that one. He's got a good eye for horror. (Is it my dad?) The cat moves from one shaft of moonlight to the next, rubs herself against the larder door like a stripper. She is the only witness to the scene that is about to ensue.

'Thunk!'

He grabs it before she has time to. A marvel to behold, a museum piece in a glass case that we circle until suddenly it dawns upon us and we blush; its leather straps yet to be tied dangling prettily, horse-ily.

The Lord is all spit and stain. His spittle laughing teeth are part and parcel of the situation. They will work on the girl's memory like hungry rats trapped inside her Freudian bowel, waiting for a shrink to smash them to pieces with his but-how-do-you-feel? hammer.

He gathers the dropped object is a dropped object and turns it over in his grinning fingers. Creative Writing class says, 'No,' because fingers cannot grin. But I say, everything has a mouth.

A slight mess of sawdust spills out onto the floor. Before coming for the vegetables, the girl had pushed her penis into her bloomers at the front, but she hadn't quite finished stuffing it big enough. She pinches her thumb and finger together and squints her eyes, which means 'just a little more.' In her greed she wipes the words 'size doesn't matter' from the mouths of all motherly lovers ever. She is not trying to care about anyone. Insecurity turns her on.

The Lord says, 'What the hell is this?' like he doesn't recognize the phallus that dawns upon the pen, the stick, the rolling pin, the baton, the cucumber or the beloved carrot when we least expect it; when we are looking the other way. Behind you! Look behind you! There might be a man there — with his mastery out.

It is all so sudden, like a peal of laughter. Like a raindrop on the surface of a river. Like a rape in a sentence. He helps himself to a fitting, right here in this very larder, circa 1700, with its fine array of lifted skirt. This is the piercing of a romance that homes in greedily on the girl's ingeniousness. She is fine ground, rising up to greet a stumbling man. She is the butter and the accidental wife.

In the Lord's mind is the start of a summer day, illuminating all the places he will clear for her to lay him down in the dust of a Faulkner novel. This one, with an imagination and a sense of humour to boot. To ground, to bent grass, to blanket. He wants to see what she plans to do with that thing. He wants her to put it in his mouth and ram it against the back of his throat until he gags sudden tears.

Other gentlemen have got erections and equally spittle-glossed teeth. They draw us in, out of the rain of cities, to a roaring fire, flanked by a row of polished maids who have been selected by the tip of the Marquis de Sade's pointer. They offer us brandy in glasses blown fat like the bellies of the men they are designed to fill. With their wet, shimmering distensions and their open-mouthed surrender they almost make gluttony sexy.

The Lord uses this moment to shove the dildo spitefully into her parched O. She is hurt. You would be too. You may have been hurt before. Is this the right time to talk about that? Is the air too flippant; the fiction too fictional? If I could cry I would, but I've seen it all before, in my imagination, while waiting for this bus or that, the whole bleeding tale dribbling down the leg of the person beside me. And I have wished tears upon myself, but the face is a desert at times, with the eyes squeezed dry of all compassion and I struggle to hold back the glitter. Let it all out! Let all the kittens out of all the bags. They will all eventually make it back to their drowning sob stories. The sweepings, the tops and tails, the waste matter, the debris floating in Hannah's sink will be clawed out in the end.

She plans to put out for the loneliest of maids, the kind you'd meet at the end of a ten-foot pole, with their hands pressed neatly into their well-ironed pockets and their mother's warnings tap-tapping on their heads. It's confusing because the girl isn't a 'strange man' or a 'man taking liberties' or a 'man with one thing on his mind.' She isn't even a man. But transcendence comes at the small price of some leather and sawdust. It's her ticket to be ridden and to ride and it makes a nice tapping gesture against her leg, while it waits while she works while she flirts. Mostly, though, she forgets it is there. Just a tucked mouse. Well, more like a rat or even the runt of a litter of kittens.

Her vagina, initially the toothless smile of a bedridden grandmother, is now undeniable erect — despite the Lord shoving her into the corner of the larder, trying to spurt sawdust onto her cervix. The cat, padding silently back to its bag of offspring, is the only witness to this anatomical contradiction.

It is late. The Lord's belly is ablaze with poems. Their flames lick his œsophagus, bringing bile to the back of his mouth. He must write something down, quickly. He must record his delight at the girl's lifted skirts, her cum-strung apron strings. He must capture the smell of leather and sawdust; the little tickle of straps.

---

There is a world outside this one. It has colour and grace. Lambs in the fields around More House bleat and maa. Out-of-season harebells fleck in blue the dense hedgerows, where two children walk carrying Granny's milk churn. A rustic scene made rusty by years of crying at not getting to have a turn under the fingers of a big-boned milkmaid. The lambs erupt — metonyms of spring on rigid, coiled legs — too skittish to hug. Into the fluffy landscape trunks poke their needles and leaves. Arching arches. Rosy roses. Leaning lupins, half-snapped by a child's meddlesome fingers. A child we shall call 'me.'

# 21

Worry is a hard sack across the girl's back. She needs to be distracted, so I have offered her the part of Woman in a Window and she has accepted it. Earlier this morning I spread photos of my favourite windows out on the table inside her trailer and she chose three: the front alcove window where my mother smeared my hand with mashed comfrey before bandaging it; the escape route window with the liver-spotted book of fairytales; and the shelf window with my melodrama and I squeezed together, in love, between the cold pane and the Laura Ashley curtains. Of these, she said it was up to me. I chose the escape route window.

She is there for a long time, the worry shifting to make room for more that is coming. The window is open-minded to the billowing fracas of the Lord's salon-styled hair. There is a rain storm. There is a quiet winter morning. There is a swallow dipping to the pull of the garden. And in the middle of all this is the great bulk of the Lord's body. He is in a state of contrition, because I have told him to be so. Unable to take his eyes off the girl in the window, he tries to describe her, stumbling over superlatives from a script that he once had memorized but has since forgotten.

The Hans Christian Andersen book on the windowsill has a hand that holds out a pair of ballet slippers. Helen and I pull imaginary paintbrushes, one for each Richard of York gave battle in vain, from imaginary pots of paint and patter across the church hall floor in piss-stained tutus. We laugh at the frilliness of the ballet teacher's commands and at our ridiculously empty hands. Is she forgetting that her little ballerinas have eyes and brains?

The girl sits at the window with her hair swirling about her bonnet-less head. Winter is inside books but threatening to come out and touch everyone and ruin everything. The rain storm was little more than filler and the swallow is in fact at this very moment darting from the eves of a chapel in Spain. That's where the winter comes in. That's what the quietness of a winter morning sounds like and here's where it is. It colours the sky a serious line across a forehead; it makes loneliness a mixed feeling; it slows down the creatures in the garden to such a degree that they cannot help but be polite.

The imaginary pot of battle-blue paint is violated by a dripping of orange brush. William. Richard. Henry. All violations. The colours of rust and gout and wounded knee. Legs eleven suggests that somebody somewhere has been amputated at the thigh. Both thighs.

Give me peace, memory. Keep me from the staircases of powerful men. This is unacceptable. This intermingling of colours, of memories, of historical figures, of window spaces and church hall floors. But it is essential. Like everything. Essential like taking a shit. Essential, my favourite, my inner being, my vanilla essence kept in a tin with half-full packets of shredded coconut, angelica and jelly diamonds. The word 'essential' has been expelled from the throat of the population like a peanut on a cough. The job of resuscitating it is a full-time one.

My rainbow is bleeding and messy and my tutu is still wet from the last joke — the joke that turned the teacher's eye into a stiff command and our bad legs into wood.

The window is open and winter is into it. It is better with the eyes closed. The wind will pass through her and take the Lord with it and deposit him in a lunatic asylum and his condition — wandering testicle — in the index of a psychology book. Her eyes are closed. She is lost inside the scene. The worry is shifting. Winter is coming to take her away and the storybook fluttering on the sill cannot prevent it. She brushes a thought that shocks her with its sharp tip, and blood wells, light coming and shifting against the hull of a ship. The relief at seeing her there in the window, at home, deadens his fear that she will leave him. He wants to shout up at her some Romeo lines, but the sky sucks at her eyes, deafens her. He rises in the house. The spirit of the witch inside him light, but hungry. Behind him Coleridge's mastiffs yelp from the pages of a library book.

The rainbow is invisible, as are the paintbrushes and the paint pots. The colours do not drip or mix. And Helen and I cannot take these imaginary games seriously. The dance teacher is angry and pushes me into one corner and Helen into another. 'Stand there and face the wall,' she says. It's still funny. I stick out my tongue and taste the wall. The laughing piss heats my leotard and tights. Until shame.

She is not sitting in the fucking windowsill. Insert Title: There is no wind and no book. It was orange and stained and the pages were musty mustard. I cannot describe it. It sits there like a woman and I cannot describe it. I just look at it and I know one thing: it is a book. He closes the doors and windows in every room in the house and he draws the drawn-on curtains. That's the point. Winter gets into the house and makes a lot of noise — a mess of noise. The point is that darkness can be found in every room of a house. Yours or mine, and even yours and even mine. She is at the window but she is too distracted to be reached with words. There is nobody in the bedroom but a book — whispering its store of stories out of the window and off on a gust of wind, sucked northward under the runners of the Ice Queen's sleigh.

I dip nothing into nothing and paint nothing. An air dance. A ridiculous command. The teacher insults our intelligence by making us dance with the air. But that is the point. It is not yet time to take a partner. We must learn to dance inside our heads first. By ourselves.

Helen, laughing inside her throat, stands in the opposite

corner and we turn slightly, slightly, to find each other's eyes. Still in their sockets. To know the joke. To have the joke. To laugh. Now *that* is dancing.

'Joey, you're in this scene. Come on.'

He's been chitty-chat-chatting with one of the back-up singers for the last half an hour. I never miss a thing.

---

The set we are standing in is my bedroom circa 1981. Two bunk beds = four children. In the centre of the room, on the floor, is a miniature guillotine, which would be used for decapitating the tips of my fingers if my fingers weren't so goddamn fast. The carpet is threadbare and cheap. I hate it. Nothing beautiful can happen here. Joey and I look towards the open window at the sound of the book's fluttering pages. We look towards stories.

'Close it! Quickly! Something might have escaped!'

There are so many unseen things happening that it is impossible to record them all. There is something rising in the house that I have started to become. A leg leaving a room. The carpet. The shifting, half-drawn curtains. A river of Lego shimmering down. A building going up. I realize. It will come down. Joey knows this as well as I do, so we close the book to keep everything in; to put the stories on pause while we pick up every single piece of Lego.

The opening of the bedroom door is the word 'stop.' It is always the word 'stop' and it always will be and that is the tragedy of being a child. Stop. Cut. Nothing is mentioned even if it is seen. It is easier to turn your head, turn your head, mother, turn your head. Can't you see that children are walking fires that adults want to stoke? Who will douse us?

'What are you doing in here?'

'Nothing.'

It is always 'nothing' but nothing is always something. To them. To you. And to me.

Joey is telling me a rhyme. 'Milk, milk, lemonade, 'round the corner chocolate-ade.' I point along with him at my nipples, my capital Y, my bum. I laugh. Other things happen. Lots. Curtains get drawn because the night has an artistic flair about it.

---

There is no-one at the window and there never has been. The book used to be there, but it has been thrown, angrily, down into the snow. When I rage I turn my bedroom into my stepfather's face and belly and spine. And then I go to work on it. Loudly.

The room behind me is a battered landscape, rained on by pieces of Lego. Red of yellow gave blue in violet. The darkness has no source. It just comes and goes to the swish of curtains and the flutter of pages. Like Joey. He understands my murderous instinct, the poison I keep inside a plastic poison ring, the picnic knife I saved and now have stored under my pillow.

There is nothing warm about the room, but we make do with the fading heat within us. Joey and I are children and that means winter likes to wrap us in its icy mantle. I expect the Snow Queen will come for him soon. When she does I will follow on her powdery trail to rescue him from becoming callous and mean like me.

'Here comes the voice of the wind. Shush. Listen. It comes whispering Hans Christian Andersen secrets into our pixie ears. Put them into your mouth. And then, out of your mouth, put them into mine.'

I go down into the garden to retrieve the snow-damp book. When the book dries, even though its spine is uneven, its stories are still straight and its girls are still girls.

# 22

'Read what you just cut. Paste it here,' says the director.

I begin to read in my reading-aloud voice. I am sure that this is where the novel used to begin. Here or under some trees in Vancouver, back in the days I thought I could write. She's alive and kicking: 'A girl in white stilettos is whining for a chocolate bar, thumping the platform's vending machine with her petite fists. The station master has had it up to here with the rudeness of kids today. He situates himself behind bars or roves about the platform with his whistle and watch. The little bitch is screeching, "Hurry up! Fucking hurry up!" at the boyfriend who hates being told what to do. It is not a matter of there will be another, but of now and this one and hurry up for fuck's sake we're going to miss the train. But the boyfriend's lanky legs just aren't lanky enough and the train pulls off without them.'

'Joey's legs are lanky enough,' says the director.

I ignore her and continue reading: 'Some teenagers are there for the sitting space alone. For the graffiti surfaces and the snogging benches. Joey listens to the clicking of the girl's shoes. She buds bruises around her left eye and on both arms are the tattoos of her boyfriend's mad hands. Joey knows her from somewhere. English class? The youth centre? A previous wank? She is beautiful and dirty, with shoplifted golden locks and a greying miniskirt. She brings to mind Tampax and stale lipstick, mugs of cold tea with lily pads of milk floating on them. Her face is a little girl's face made up by a whore.

'Her boyfriend has left to buy cigarettes. She is pissed off that they have to wait for the next train. It is Sunday and cold and boring. She limps over to the shelter with blistered fuck, fuck, fuck feet. Joey watches her from the sanctuary of his hooded sweatshirt. He is slumped uncomfortably into the corner of the shelter, desperately trying to ignore the spite of winter.

'Joey is also trying to ignore thoughts of the inevitable beating he is going to get once he gets home, young man. This morning his mother asked him a stupid question — he can't even remember what is was now — and he told her to fuck off. When she remained with her head poking around his bedroom door, he lobbed the nearest object to hand — a large wad of Plasticine — at her. It hit her on the temple.'

'Fine,' says the director. 'Let's shoot this scene.'

The station is in Deal, so I ask the set decorator to find a crisp packet that has lost its colour under a pile of soggy leaves, and the sound technician to poke his microphone into a vending machine to record the 'thunk' of a Cadbury's Fruit and Nut.

'OK. Joey. Get up, then walk towards the waiting room, but carry on past it.' (The director is beginning (beginning?) to piss me off because it's my scene and in my scene Joey just sits and observes.) 'Whatever happens just keep walking. Don't turn around or try to do anything to help.'

'Help?'

'Wait!' I run in from off-set and pull Joey's hood up over his head. 'Now. Slouch.' He does. The camera begins to roll.

Joey follows the director's instructions, while trying to look as slouchy and sullen as possible, for me. (I think I love him).

Just as he is about to reach the waiting room door, it flings open and the blonde comes running through, screaming at the top of her lungs for help. It's a Sunday. No-one is around. The rest of the cast and crew wait behind the camera, smoking, sipping from Styrofoam, keeping their eyes peeled for inconsistencies. The stilettos are white. The hair is blonde. Tick.

Right on the girl's tail is a man dressed up like a football mascot with clown feet and great fluffy claws. He is supposed to be a wolf, but his head has fallen off, revealing the actor who usually plays the Lord sweating inside.

Joey, acting on instinct, sticks out a foot and trips the wolf-man up.

The girl, thinking the scene is still rolling, has already reached the train bridge, but as she scrambles up the stairs she also trips — like someone has choreographed the whole thing.

'Shit! We'll have to shoot it again,' she shouts, examining her bloodied knee and wishing she was a kid so that she could cry. 'It's these bloody shoes!' She hurls one across the platform at the wolf-man.

The director has got Joey by the arm and is shaking him. 'What the fuck was that?! Can't you follow a simple instruction?!'

Joey fingers her and walks off-set, taking the shoe with him. He is ready to be born into a different narrative. He wants to team up with the girl and make something happen — something like revenge. He's opting for a period piece, dripping in daddy blood.

'Joey!' I have followed him out to the train-station parking lot. I'm out of breath when I catch up to him. 'Joey. Look. Do you want to be the murderer or the lover? I had you pegged as the murderer, but maybe that's not your cup of tea. Have you got a preference? Am I assuming too much here?'

'I thought this was a porn film?'

'It was. At first. But things just keep getting in the way. I think it's best we just shoot whatever happens — porn or not — and just see where it gets us in the end. I liked your mini-rebellion back there. Because whoever the hell thought the Lord in a wolf outfit would fit in this novel needs her head checked. It's weird and it's stupid. Look. You've got the shoe. Do you want to wear it or use it as a weapon?'

'A weapon? A shoe a weapon? Wear it? But there's only one.'

'Don't worry about that. The costume designer has white stilettos coming out the yin yang. She usually works in porn.'

'Neither, thanks. I just want to go home.'

I don't understand Joey one bit at this exact moment. At this exact moment he is acting like a robot-zombie, out of my control. Damn.

---

The girl looks up at the ceiling in the kitchen as if she can see the sound of hounds over the body of the maid above. It is the maid's first time, being only fifteen, a good Christian, and new at More House as of this morning. The girl's anger fishes bile up onto the banks of her tongue.

There the anger. There the boiling point and overflow. The frothy bastions of creeps spill onto this page, this heaving lung. Starlings are never cooed at. Gates found dangling off a single hinge are never fixed. The hardest rage to bear is the kind that attaches itself to small matters. Where's the fucking plug!? What fucking thing is stuck down the fucking plughole!? What kind of sticks and picks and hooks can get it out? Fury glues. Rage gets into crevices and hardens. The stench fills the alleys and conduits of a screaming match. Of your body. Your great mouth widens and spits teeth.

The girl's rage is creating an ugly pie. Hannah looks up from her pastry, slaps her hands down onto the floured table, and says, 'What *is* your problem, young lady? Would you rather it was you up there?'

The rage glistens a bright moment and then fades. It is alive, but resting.

'Perhaps. But not in the way that you think.'

'In what way then? What other bloody way is there?'

'As the Lord himself.'

Hannah laughs. Contagiously. Begrudgingly, the girl catches the humour and is sick with it too.

'Give me a break, love. Why would a pretty young lass like you want to be a great goat of a man? It's just not right.'

---

The first time I was on my back a deer drowned in Okanagan Lake, filtered up through the layers of my mother's dreaming head. Behind her temples a silent movie caught on the cog of a still: two skinny teenagers fiddling with a condom. The juice from my popped cherry was so great that I drowned too.

In the morning the deer's corpse was found on shore by a boy scout. He had been hoping for a human, but a deer was exciting enough. He prodded at its winter-starved belly with a piece of driftwood.

# 23

The girl stands on the threshold of her parents' house for the last time. It is the same fire that kills and the same water that washes the quiet body. Chest still. Chest at the end of the charred bed opening for the first time its gifts. Tired hands finishing one more line along the clicking knitting, needling one more hem on a tablecloth.

Mother didn't know that she needed glasses. The perching kind. Beyond the smoky reek of tragedy, the chest smells of her. Smell cannot be written into a will, but whoever gets the deep scent of the mother's hair and cheek and neck and stuffs it down into the back corner of the bottom drawer gets all the riches.

The graveyard is on the top of a hill. The girl lurches upward through deep, fresh snow, her hands drooping snowdrops. There the two graves are side by side, like her parents' beds when they were alive. The weather has the back of his hand poised, ready to strike the girl on the crown of her crowning memories, which come now, with their fresh, wet heads, pricking tears like stitches.

All the hills come together and flicker. One for the other. There is no knowing where the girl's foot will place itself next, because snow can fall quietly on any of the hills inside my head. It rounds and holds the world together. I dig one grave and then I dig another and push her thumping parents into them. Under the hill. The dancers have all gone.

Standing there at the overripe gate — one hinge holding everything together — she sends her rage drifting over the dark hills, over the entire country. The mother and the father are tapping against their coffin lids. Or perhaps it is that horse clattering by? On its rounds. Round the hills. Over the dancers. She pulls at the ribbons of her white maypole dress that has been touched by too many hands and out of it fall hawthorn blossoms and thorns. It is as white as May inside the chest at the foot of her mother's bed. Out of the soot the contents of the chest come, heaving with asthma.

The girl is pushing through the pages of an Emily Brontë novel. Climbing the sublime for the sake of saying she has. I have no reason to put her in black booties and hustling skirts, to keep her hair pulled back off her face so that stray bits can dance in her breath. I can keep the clichés back with sticks and hooks. Shove into the parts that never see the light the flakes of past rages. The slightest breeze could easily carry them off, but the air in the body is always thick and dark and sluggish. No strength to push. The flecks of dirty emotion remain as a coating on even the loveliest of English afternoons, when there is not a cloud in the sky, and the shade of an old oak tree is never more than a few footsteps away. Shall we take a walk?

I have no strength to ask where the anger originates. It isn't that simple anyway. We die with our rages intact and still sticky. I cannot locate the source. There is no anger remover, no fury uprooter, no memory shooter. It's what gets a girl up a steep hill, at night, through the deep snow, with More House a sore spot on the horizon, occasionally turned to and glared at, huffed at, spat at.

When her parents sent her to work for the Lord they secretly hoped that she would come home with her womb stocked blue. Good. But she doesn't because the Lord's factory runs smoothly, coughing white steam all over Yorkshire. (Or is that Just Outside London? Or are we still going with Granny, More House, More? Call the cartographer.) And like steam does, it dissipates. The babies are prammed out to the barren wives of farmers around these parts. The wives spoon their husbands in moonlit beds. Zero poster. And the new spoon, the teaspoon, fits snugly between them.

Both parents seem dead enough, but perhaps it should only be the mother who dies? After all, she doesn't have a fancy man to run to, who can mop her brow and present her with bowls of sexy fruit (especially raspberries, her all time favourite, with cream, eaten messily). She has left people behind. A baby. Yes. A baby. My uncle. Wait! These are the girl's parents. It is a matter of getting over the scenes that plague me. Take Dora at the kitchen sink filling her lungs with Bizet, for example. She is so stuck there. Freeze-framed for my imagination to lick and lick forever. The flowers in her garden with their speaking faces turned up to her grey, sick one with expectancy and a little something spiritual. She sings to them through the morphine fug, reassuring them that she will be back in the morning with the water hose to pour opera onto their pistils and stamens; reassuring them that, as their mother, she will love them until they wilt and crisp and she must pull them up and drag them over to the compost heap.

---

'OK,' says the director. 'Her parents are dead. Fine. But why is this important? You also seem to be crossing a lot into my territory. I'm making the period piece, remember? And you the porno. Or am I missing something?'

'I'm having trouble focusing. I didn't sleep well last night. I had some nasty dreams. Coffins with live people inside. A burning house. Singed tippy toes and such.'

'Oh. So . . . that means you've got something else in mind now?'

'Yes. Let's just shoot whatever happens and then edit it later. The audience can catch our drift and then just sail right on down into the breezy spring copse where my brothers and sisters are still playing.'

'I'm not sure I know what you mean by that?'

'Look. Take that guy over there. Hey! What's your name?'

'Me? Steven. With a *v*.'

'OK. Come here. And stand like so. Good. Here, put this around your neck, like a necklace, just as a reminder of who you are. OK. Great. Now, cameras . . . and . . . ACTION!'

In the same week that the girl's parents die, the butler at More House loses at a game of hangman. He leaves behind a corpse, a rope, a small will, and a son — Solomon. The funeral is nothing special.

'Look sad. Like you've killed yourself but now you regret it.'

Steven with a *v* is a fine actor. Trained at the Royal Shakespeare Company under the lights of my father and able to command a person to stop everything and listen. He has lovely hair too. Wavy and grey. Like my father's. He's not my father though. He's only one of my father's shadows. The dark one that my brother would like to slash through with light.

I bring him in and I kill him off. It's a short affair, nothing to get too emotional about. We need him only for his son. The dashing young one over there ('Yes, come on over') who catches the girl by the plural skirts and spins her to the window so she can watch his feet pass and throw down her initials. (Joey isn't keen on being either the murderer or the lover of his own mother so I've no other choice but to find a replacement. This isn't a problem. They flutter out to infinity, my paper boys.)

After the funeral, the girl walks over to Solomon — who looks familiar, like Joey but with blue-coloured contact lenses — and kisses him on the cheek. Then she passes a few words into his ear, but they are words reserved for those in mourning and cannot be repeated here. He smiles.

The scene gets cut at this place. The girl and Solomon laugh their real laughs and smooth their real hair. And then we start the snowblower again and the clapper shouts the word 'ACTION!'

'Are you alright?'

'Yeah.'

'What are you going to do?'

'I don't know.'

'You can stay here, you know?'

'Can I sleep in your bed with you?'

'Perhaps.' I'm in the corner of the girl's eye, nodding wildly, thumbs up. 'No, yes. Yes, you can.'

I turn to the director and throw out my arms dramatically.

'And there you have it!' I say. 'Things happening!'

# 24

Joey has been told to wait in Mr. Nobody's study with his pants down, bent over the desk. He waits too long for my liking. My brother and I have been told to do the same thing. Our pajama skins are around our ankles, leaving my fig and his carrot exposed, while our stepfather is somewhere else in the house, masturbating over just the thought of us waiting for him. My brother whispers a word in my ear and at once I whisper it to Joey: 'Run!'

On the wall in front of Joey is a map of South America — that great Brazilian jungle split by a questing blue line that keeps its lips against the Atlantic. The space to film is large and into it I fly a plane escorting a camera crew down. The fact that there is snow, which is white, and the thunder of chased animals means that this moment means nothing.

He speaks to his pants, now spare cloth around his ankles: 'Cover me,' he says. The speed of the needle takes place and makes a wage for a team of smoking, joking factory women. The pants were put at the end of his bed after they came home from shopping in Canterbury with the tag still on and the first thought he had as he bit into the plastic was that teeth were fragile. And there were scissors in reach. It's a matter of looking around you. And he does. He sees Brazil with all the green of the world blaring off its back; an untouched cup of tea with a lily pad of brooding milk concealing its bright tannin; and the dreaded newspaper, that at times is a substitute for the father or at least can suggest his recent or future presence. It is even a shroud for a dead body. One that has been cold since the early hours of this novel. There is no question about what Joey should do. Run.

Instead he just stays there, bent over the desk, frozen — with a draught that has gotten past the draught excluder tickling his bottom. He is a Bosch-boy giving his arse to a dealer, burning shamefully under an historian's magnifying glass. Horribly, horribly exposed.

Joey's obedience frustrates me. Faced with a view of the Amazon River he cannot see that the door to Mr. Nobody's study is a mouth that opens out onto liberty, onto water full of whales. If he could just look at it from the perspective of the land versus the water, there would be no question. He would run.

'There is no reason at all — ever — to hit a child,' my mother says. She stands behind the shoulders of sons and daughters and nudges them towards the judge lovingly. I love her lowered hand. It makes me another chamomile tea and opens the taps for my bath. The sound of the water means we are all preparing for bed. All the girls. All the pajamas.

I add, just to make Mrs. Nobody — who has entered the room like it is her first day at an AA meeting (she enters all rooms in this manner) — feel better, that 'a good man is hard to find.' And that is certainly an allusion to Flannery O'Connor's *A Good Man is Hard to Find*. Just the title. It's true that I wasn't really thinking when I wrote that, but punish me, hit me, and I promise I'll behave.

'There is no reason at all,' my mother repeats, pulling Joey's pants up for him and pushing him gently forward away from this page. 'Run!'

---

Steven left home to look for work. With his real head kept on a spike inside his fake butler head, he took a carriage to More House like a lord might. He left behind stained paintbrushes soon to be picked up by the imaginations of goody-two-shoes ballet students and their inane rainbow exercises. Face the corner! He left behind a trail of half-finished canvasses that dreamed of being hung. Nobody ever saw these pictures. Perhaps 'painter' was just a hat he wore. A hat full of lies. Still, I spent ages in a shop in London picking out paintbrushes of the right thickness. I bought two. One for the wide sky stroking. The other for letting us know what the hell that is. I worried that he would reject my gift, but he didn't. He even painted me into his will: *to the writer of my life I leave a character — my son, Solomon.*

But the paintbrushes couldn't keep him alive. Two wooden sticks with some horsehairs at their ends? What was I expecting?

Steven had been known to hit Solomon. Emerging from the sleepy fug of a hangover to find that his son had once again neglected his chores, would send Steven into a rage. He couldn't understand the laziness of kids today and had never imagined that any son of his would end up hanging around with a bunch of thugs. Kids today were always ending up in the local newspaper, most recently for having set fire to a sack of weeping kittens, but usually for having turned on each other with their boots and knives. Solomon swore that he wasn't with them when any of these events look place, but to Steven anyone under the age of twenty was to be considered guilty. Even the girls. In fact, the girls were sometimes worse.

Unlike Joey's stepfather, who got aroused when spanking children, or my stepfather, who is a thinly disguised version of my real stepfather and also got aroused, Steven only hit Solomon out of rage. Only.

I am preparing a list of excuses for them all and when they are ready I will wrap them in a pretty handkerchief — just to soften the hypocrisy (as if hypocrisy isn't soft and flabby enough already!) — and I will give them to my mother and yours. Maybe Mr. Nobody was hit by a masturbating house master when he was at boarding school? Maybe a combination of high blood pressure, stress and drunkenness trigger Steven's uncontrollable rages? Maybe my stepfather wasn't loved enough by his militant mother? Who knows?

No, but really, who does know? Who knows what goes through a person's head when they hit a child? What flash of genius? What sparkling solution presents itself inside a light bulb? 'Ah ha! The answer was right under my nose all this time! How stupid of me! I will bash the truancy out of my son's bottom! I will whack the obstinacy right off my daughter's face! I will use this stick to drive the sass out of all my children! And, then, I will knock their heads together to make sure they never forget who's boss around here!'

Joey runs away from Mr. Nobody's study — straight into the liberating unpredictability of this movie, into stardom — but Solomon, met by the suddenness of his father's suicide, has no need anymore for escape routes or poison rings, and so he stays put. Joey's luckier half.

This is no consolation though. It is much easier to mourn the death of a good father than it is to remember how many times you wished death upon a bad one. The guilt gets greedy — requiring a drip hooked up to a lifetime's supply of alcohol or drugs or meaningless fuckery or a combination of all three. Solomon is no easy friend. The girl is at this moment trying to clear a space for him in her heart's compassion department. There is nowhere else to put him. He needs to be tucked in at night by a nurse with giant, milk-filled tits. He needs a concussion.

# 25

The girl has agreed to meet with me to go over the anatomy of this film. Between us I am hoping we can make some sense out of this mess. I have her by the hand, but it doesn't mean that together we can't stray. We stray a great deal, in fact. Like our mothers. Into the fields around these parts. To the end of the garden to smoke cigarettes. Into the cancer ward with our cells refusing to believe in reincarnation. Off somewhere. Gone out.

We leave wasps battling honey water to replace us. A great silence lurks, but we evade it under our hooded capes — coloured green like the trees that fuss us.

I tell her that I would like to interview her, but she says that talking to me is irritating because I don't really listen. 'There isn't much in the way of words around here, anyway,' she says.

'What do you mean?! This is a book! And I *do* listen!'

I want to get to the bottom of her complaint. I can handle it and tell her to give it to me straight up. She has looked carefully inside my head, and, luckily, says that my imagination has potential, but that it tends to stop when things are about to get good. I cry when she says this because I know she is right. I don't think I can be much of a writer if my own characters don't even believe I can get them where they need to go, wearing accurate fashions and transported in the right make of carriage.

'There are a few gestures in the back if you want me to go and get them?' she says. She is trying to be kind, but sarcasm is easier for her. She's had a tough life, don't forget. But I don't care. I feel defensive. I see that I am not getting anywhere with such a contrary, unpredictable character. Somebody yells 'She's over here!', and then that's about all the time she has for me for this whole thing is a sham and I am ashamed.

'Wait!' I shout after her. 'Talk and I promise just to listen.' She stops. 'OK,' she says, beginning her story with a small curtsey like any good actress, which immediately makes me regret having called her back.

'I bent down to pick up the fallen penis, but when I bent the Lord bent too. You must have written him arms that were just that *little bit* longer than mine'(I look down at my notes. Yes, she's right. Next to the Lord's name I have written 'long arms') 'so he snatched it up before I could.'

'Did it hurt?'

'Yes. It was dry as a bone in there. I regretted having made it so big. I even bled.'

'Did you scream?'

'No. Nobody told me to scream.'

'Well, as an actress you should have taken a scream or two as a given, no?'

'I usually work as a mime artist.'

'Really? How interesting.' Shit. Who hired this girl? I look down at my notes once more. Next to the girl's name I see my own. Shit.

'Well for this film it's best that you forget your mime skills.'

She pastes on a big creepy smile, nods, and gives me the finger. Undeniably skillfully.

If the larder window had been open the sound of carriage wheels (see Jane Austen for make and description) on gravel would have had everybody's ears pricked up like little pricks. But we're not in a real larder, we're on a film set and the world and the sound technician are too little with us today.

Beside us the actors who play the girl's mother and father are being shot. Their lines flash in and fade out: 'Stick it up your fancy woman why don't you keep your mouth shut you old hag if I hadn't married what the hell do you think I married it's fine for who on earth?!' The scene ends with the mother leaving the father to re-erect the set she has scandalously kicked down. At one point the poor man is forced to go chasing after the cardboard walls of his own house that tumble off over the California landscape, getting dust in their net curtains.

It is almost time for the girl's next scene, the window scene, in which she must act sad and press her forehead against a windowpane until she gets brain-freeze. She is smoking appropriately and of course. Her manner is aloof now and her answers are mumbled and brief. I predicted that our momentary lapse into intimacy would be short lived, but that's because, for this sentence, I am a negative cow.

I look over my notes: Where? The north. When? In 1814. Who was the father? Some dashing lord of the glen in his riding boots with whistling in fashion. Battle is her favourite colour. And there is nothing she likes better than a cheese sandwich with a glass of red wine. The cock was her idea and came at a time in her life when her sex sagged nosily into every I-won't-take-no-for-an-answer. And that was the summer of '14. Everyone was swinging something between their legs. But like all loose eras, 1814 was followed by a backlash. The whole village decided that Hannah was a witch and wanted to burn her alive, but not wanting to appear barbaric, decided against it at the last minute. She came into work on Monday morning with black toes.

The girl also tells me that lavender grows in abundance in these parts and wafts its calm through the windows at More House. I can literally see the scent rising up her movie-star hams. If I turned her around you would be able to see eyeliner seams lick sexily up her imaginary stockings. It's wartime. What's a woman to do?

By the end of the interview she has her arms crossed over her lung cancer. Her eyes roll themselves all the way to section 'M' of the dictionary and come to rest at the word 'Marble.' Her sullenness is almost as bad as Joey's evil streak. She likes drama and it is obvious that she'd rather be back on the set trying to stop her mother from smashing a tray over her father's head.

It's not the tray I bought a few weeks ago at Value Village that has a Chinese cat on it, but I wish it could be. It's a nondescript tray. That means a tray that isn't worthy of adjectives. Tray. That's all it gets. It wouldn't hurt him because he's been in the pub all afternoon and is numb from stout and bitterness. And he deserves it anyway because it's her birthday and all he can do is throw sugar at her, like she is still a child, hopeful, ambitious, capable of doing anything at all, bouncing around on the moon in her astronaut suit singing arias. She is not the opera singer she so confidently believed in her teenage heart she would grow up to be. She is a nurse and a housewife. For the performance of a lifetime, the highly popular show *Five Children Crammed Up My Uterus by My High-School Sweetheart,* all she gets is a box of fucking chocolates. (Another reason the girl wants to get back on set). Once her children have wormed their way onto her lap and have eaten all her chocolates, she will have absolutely nothing to put on her resumé.

The mother is momentarily distracted from her unhappiness by the smell of lavender coming from around these parts. The garden beckons. Look at the pretty maids. They seem to be speaking. She is on the verge of smiling, but not wanting to waste any more wrinkles on the road to nowhere, she pulls herself back into the self-righteous comfort of disappointment, and goes back to beating her husband.

I am actually relieved when the girl ambles back listlessly into the scene allowing me to shuffle off to my own trailer. Who shuffles? Girls who think that they're ugly? Who ambles? Or has her arms akimbo? Or carries a pomegranate in her pocket, that she plans to offer to a listless girl who stands in a doorway with her arms akimbo too? Get the pomegranate out of the pocket, because it's nothing more than an expensive word and stop bothering to describe arms because they're not interesting. And what's wrong with the verb 'to walk'? 'Walk' is a fine word. So is 'said.' But I'll take two dozen 'ambles', a crate of 'gasped', a few 'exclaimed' and a whole basket of 'replied.' That should keep things original. Whoever would have thought replacing overused words with under-used ones was all it would take to write a novel? But wait! For a low price, short-term rental, they'll also throw in a couple of 'groans' and one chilling 'screamed.' And that's what'll seal the deal.

I raise my voice at the other side of my split personality. So sarcastic. So cheap and lonely. 'Shut up and write!'

# 26

I've made the decision to get raped in a sentence. It won't immunize me from the memory, but it might make it easier to stuff a few more excuses into this beautiful, bulging handkerchief.

The word *rape* is a strong one. It gets batted around from one boxing ring to the next like a lightweight dancing out of the path of a heavyweight. I don't give the word much clout. It's a public word, accessible to anyone, whatever age or sex, and has a definition that can be found in any dictionary. It pops out of the mouths of anchormen and professors. It appears on certain police paperwork. It is also the word for an oil, a crop, a gloriously yellow hill that I ride past on my horse. It cannot then follow that this word can signify an experience that only I had. Or only my friend had. Or only that person over there had. Or only you had. We do not permit the policeman to carry this word in his mouth like a wad of chewing gum. We do not permit the anchorman to tell us that the rapist has been caught and incarcerated. He is not a man. The experience is not an event, like a concert or a conference. We do not think of it while it is happening. Only afterwards. Years afterwards, while we are putting down the letters *R*, *A*, *P* and *E* onto a Scrabble board. Years later, when he's married and has kids and is a professional with high standing in the local community; when his jail sentence is finished and his criminal record is collecting dust down at the police station; when the skin of a lover suddenly rubs us the wrong way, or we find ourselves doing things we don't know why we are doing — things that are dangerous and wrong, with people we don't even like. That is when the rape happens.

I am writing about rape because I am in a negative mood today. I can't shake the news. I can't get out of the plastic bag that he put her in. The river that bloated her and then pushed her to shore. The birds that sweetly attempted to bury her with leaves or the insects that milked her of blood and identity.

They planned everything — how much whiskey they would need to pour for me before I would let them both fuck me at the same time; what to say to get me to come back, alone, to their house; what to cook me for dinner. They wrote an ingredients list, they used a calculator and they drew a chart. Then they pre-meditated on their yoga mats for the whole afternoon before driving over to my house to pick me up.

I give them this title in retrospect. Their dirty wolf whiskers, that sniffed out my low self-worth, were barely visible at the time. I gave them all I had to offer so that they would like me. A murder is always a murder, but a rape is sometimes a 'good time.' Had by all. A right laugh. Their madness on my madness, slipping over the surfaces that were neither mine nor theirs, but of another world. I hit the ceiling and stayed there, floating calmly, humming softly down to my body below.

---

I let them fondle me because *fondle* is a word I don't like, a word reserved for perverted uncles and friends' dads. There is a disaster that is being reported live from the television by a woman with a flaccid bowtie. It is a disaster. They say they'll make me one of my very own to wear when I'm walking along the dusty highway with the eyes of truckers running out of time before I can rouse them up the back of my skirt.

They call me in the afternoon and invite me for dinner. I am wanted. Hooray! 'Look pretty' is their only request. The dress I pick out is my mother's and is old fashioned in retrospect, but the early '90s allowed a few things to slip by unnoticed.

Not accustomed to this sort of adult thing, I find it difficult to choose a dress. In the end I pick the longest one.

The first thing they do, once they've shoved a plateful of spaghetti down my pelican gullet, is douse me in whiskey. I am a temple erected and situated carefully *in situ*. My flames leap so high they can see my blue soul, so they put me in the shower where I quickly reincarnate as a goat. They come in with me, just to make sure I clean myself properly, and then I see us, three soap slippery dancers, goats hoofing and rutting a cum stain, and I know who I am. I am fuck drunk and full of thigh meat, officer.

The next thing I see is that the entire bed is me and that these goats are in fact speaking English. And there, if I look closely, horns bud and break off with neat clicks. Just to bud again. These devils' smiles are warm and at me sweetly and like a cloister I am ready to receive their sin, because I am this bed and these are my four legs and these are my mattress stains.

---

For years afterwards I am a 'goer.' The news spreads through the small town, passed from one drag of a filched cigarette to the next, and all the little boys run to their windows when I pass to see what one of my type looks like. Whispered along teen lines throughout the town run the details of my performances. I go well. I go with anyone. I go in any place. I fit the description. I fit snugly between shame and lust. I fit neatly into beds and cars with boys from all sorts of Christian denominations, who drop me off afterwards outside a home that shouldn't be called a home because it is little more than a shelter.

# 27

The Lord's bed is Granny's. She is propped up by a gaggle of goose pillows with her large teacup sloshing tea that she drinks from the saucer like her saucy cat that she named Pushkin, for reasons I am too young to understand. What sits beside her is a husband. Propped also. Hands resting on his flabby paunch, smiling like a village idiot.

I wanted to build the Lord a rich Turkish set, but Granny's bed is less expensive and has ample room for a man and a maid or two, and will suffice.

I keep picking up images that are dirty. A concerned American mother is always there with a napkin telling me to 'drop it!' but I'm convinced that a little rubbing will make anything into a gem. The dog shit on my fingers is making her wretch, but I'll lick it off if she gets any closer with her tongs and her rubber gloves and her pursed lips.

Stop! Drop it! This has nothing to do with mattresses, headboards, four-posters, all of Marilyn, or sheets tucked in so tightly they wind the sleeper. There he is. See the Lord sleeping like a baby cliché. Raise the sash and flood his body with sunlight. Do disturb him. He has kept Grace awake all night. She rises now to counter his drooping, and slips quietly to her chores. The room is off limits. We can look, but we can't. Stop! Don't cross the threshold of the room. It is out of bounds to children, who should not be heard through ear plugs or closed doors or ever.

The girl's bed is thin to fit her. It has an under-the-bed and things are stashed there. Never look under a person's bed because what you find will never turn you on as much as it does them. Those perverts. A mother's fingers catch something loose to worry over in the quiet of that hour right before the kids get home from school. Nosy cow.

The girl guards her cock wearing the mask of a Doberman (my stepfather's). Selfish and scared, she is always thinking ahead to scenes of theft. The girl doesn't want any of the other maids to touch anything that is hers, and nor, quite frankly, do they.

Dead set on having something happen, she straps her penis into place and tucks it into her bloomers. There it sits like a bold child at the front of a classroom saying 'Please Miss, I know the answer, Mi-iss, Ple-ase!' She wants to be chosen by the Lord so that she can get him back, but he has been picking everyone *but* her. How can she and Joey employ their strategy without getting the Lord alone, in Granny's bed, helplessly sandwiched between Granny and her husband, if possible (because that will make me laugh)?

What is the plan? Joey, mature enough, strong enough, not a fetus or a newborn, enters the room and catches his father around the waist as he is trying to climb over Granny to get back into bed after taking a piss. Her tea spills, which really makes her mad, but that's a good thing because rage makes her prettier and less in need of my mother's makeup bag. Joey pulls the Lord's arms behind his back and pins them tightly. His father is naked. Good. The girl knocks — not wanting to anger Granny. 'Come in,' Granny coos through her wolf whiskers, and the girl enters the bedroom holding a large knife. She stands in front of the Lord with the knife raised above her head fighting off slats of morning light with its spiteful teeth. Her eyes glisten with the spittle of trauma and fear. Joey is screaming at her, 'Do it, Mum! Do it! For fucksake!'

In line with the plot that I left him in charge of, we are back with the theme of revenge. Oh, brother! I'm not a Scorpio or a man and need to take a closer look at the feel of the line. Here. Run your finger along this. Can you feel it? No? No, here. Right here. Can you feel it now? It's trying to loosen up a bit so it can twist off and float away in the warm water — fæces off an animal's coat — if the American mother will let it.

She hands her son the knife, stands on the bed and lifts her skirts up over her waist, tucking them into her apron to hold them up. Granny is forced to budge over to her husband's side. Happy to have her, having been deprived, not only of sex, but of any human touch for years now, his deflating heart farts out a puff of love.

The girl's cock is erect, as per usual, and sticks right out in line with the Lord's mouth. 'Perfect!' says Joey, nicking the skin of his father's neck in his excitement.

'I'm going to put this giant cock in your mouth and then you're going to suck it until you drool like a baby and the pain in your jaw is so strong that it makes you cry. Sound good?'

'This is ridiculous!' says the Lord.

'Do what she shez!' shouts the director, chewing on a mouthful of something from Starbucks.

'Look, just cut the scene. Let me try it first. I don't think that thing will even fit in my mouth. It'll do more than make me cry. It'll choke me to death.'

The Lord opens his mouth as wide as it will go and tries to put it around the cock. It's not as big as it looks and he manages to get it halfway in his mouth when suddenly he gags, pulls back and hurls a slopping spray of vomit all over the girl, the bed, Joey's hand and arm, and Granny's breakfast tray.

'OK. From the top,' says the director.

---

Granny isn't happy with any of this. (Or any of that, to be honest.) I am only eight years old and miss my parents, but there's no use getting into bed with the old bat. Her tray is a lovely weight on her and will not take kindly to being shifted, even when covered in vomit.

Let's take this scene elsewhere.

# 28

The photos are of Granny in her sexy thirties with her four boys on Dover Beach. Look! There's father, on a deckchair with a burnt nose. Jolly good fun. And that's war. A Portuguese man of, swept onto the beach. A miscarriage crisping in the rays of August. Sand in the cheese and tomato sandwiches, and this is the one without cheese, and this is the one without crusts. One of the boys is all freckles and grin. He waves at a ship taking soldiers across the channel on this calm and delightful Sunday afternoon.

The photographs are filling the album so that we must all look at the doctor on holiday with his boys. With the wife and the pipe and the deckchair stripes. Gulls on a hot tip that the back of the pink hotel will be opening its kitchen doors at approximately 1400 hours, hover and bitch.

There is something so beautiful in the sky. It is a cloud. A cloudy cloud. Joey is walking along Dover seafront with a whole list of tarts and cakes on his mind. 50P for a cream puff. 75 for an éclair. Donkeys are receiving hay from the cupped palms of gleefully terrified children. There are four boys on the beach circling a deckchair, making the wa-wa of Indians. It is so 1950s of them. Joey wants to play with them. He jumps down from the promenade into the sand on knobbly knees. He is wearing grey shorts and one of his socks has lost its elastic and consequently its grip on his leg. On joining them with his own splendid headdress and moccasins, the brothers' circling slows to a halt, causing papa to look up through his pipe smoke at the scene. 'Here's another boy to play with lads. Let him join you.' One of the brothers is in a mood and runs off to dig. It's reasonable. The others let Joey trail after them over their beach territory.

They find some crabs and dash their flesh out with rocks. They have taken their sandals and socks off and have left them over by the towels and the mother of the towels. She is reading a book. Get a little closer and it is obvious that what she is reading is a story about a talking crab who gets his brains dashed out by four howling Indian stereotypes, who in soft, soft moccasin quietness, manage to corner him in his own swimming pool. The last thing he sees is a dagger of god's light hitting the English Channel, which is marvellous. It is up to Miss Marple to remove the fake headdresses, to wipe the clownish war paint off these hooligans and find out once and for all *Who Murdered the Crab?*

The play of the boys and their new friend causes Granny to raise her head and offer an unseen oh-isn't-childhood-lovely smile. But the smile turns on a whiff of atmospheric grey that clouds, momentarily, the jolly good fun of the afternoon as she notes her second born sulking in the shallows. Out in the channel a ship of soldiers, having waved goodbye to bastard children and sore, sobbing girlfriends, are below deck, waving gambling hands like fans.

Once they are far enough down the beach, small and summery behind a wall of heat, Joey feels it is safe to talk. He tells the boys that he once saw a dead woman.

'You're lying,' says the tallest, which also means the eldest.

'No, I'm not. I swear to God I've seen a dead woman before.'

'Was she completely dead or almost dead?'

'Completely.'

'How do you know?'

'She had the heel of a shoe screwed into her head.' Joey imitates turning a shoe like a screwdriver. The boys grimace and wow. (The special effects guy is waving frantically at me from off scene, but I ignore him. Keep the camera rolling. We don't have time or money to change the details now.)

'Did you kill her?'

---

The doctor is folding up his deckchair and putting his camera away in its case. In his mind is a nurse. She has written him a poem, but he is too rational to understand what the bloody hell it means. The only thing he is sure of is that her white uniform, which she always places so carefully on the floor at the end of the examining table, makes her look sexy. But, this is Sunday. Family time.

The poem is good. She will go on to publish a short collection of similar works, but then will have her writing dreams dashed on the rocks of her husband's demand that she pursue a less masculine 'hobby.'

The doctor's stethoscope has somehow ended up under the bed of one of the four boys. It will not be found by the worrying fingers of their mother in that lulling and dangerous afternoon hour. Joey watches the family load their car. A donkey. The car is running away up the hill. He gathers the broken crab pieces and lobs them into the sea.

# 29

Mr. Nobody, when he used to be a real man, was a Northern Ireland street corner and gun. He won't let Joey forget this fact. Over breakfast, while Joey gulps back milk and anger, Mr. Nobody lectures.

The creaking winter speaks volumes as it fingers his fatigues. Darting through a city I have never visited is a van painting a face in its back window. Half ghost, half human. Strong tea is poured into the lid of a flask and cupped by cold hands. Last night two old women, one jittery, the other wobbling on bloated ankles — wearing the usual silk headscarves — gave sandwiches to some British soldiers. The glass was ground so fine and stirred in so nicely with the egg and mayonnaise that it wasn't noticed until all six soldiers shit blood.

Joey looks out the kitchen window. He sees the girl on the front lawn beating a rug. She looks angry. Joey wants to go out and give her a hand, but the storyteller is still working his magic. 'Where's that gun at now?' Joey thinks. 'Where's the bastard hidden it?' Which brings John Lennon to the window with a concerned look on his face. He gives peace a chance and flowers emerge from his mouth, butterflies and bees, which have the potential to sting.

'Joey! Listen to this one. You've not heard this one before.'

But that is not true. Joey has heard every single one of his stepfather's stories — more than once.

Two birds out for a shag find their way up a pole. Tarred and feathered. It is November. Their names are kept out of the paper. Mr. Nobody cuts them both out. It isn't as bad as people had expected, because the tar acted as insulation. They had turned up outside the barracks wearing their older sisters' dresses concealed beneath long winter coats with the words 'wanna shag?' written all over their bloody faces, lads. It was an IRA decision to tar and feather the cunts in good medieval fashion and then none of the girls in those parts dated a British soldier for a while.

Mr. Nobody adds that afterwards the girls didn't regret a thing. 'They'll do anything for a bit of English cock,' he says. This story makes Mr. Nobody laugh the most. Joey fiddles with the crumbs on his breakfast plate. Ground glass cuts his thoughts. And then there is a nose bleed.

A line of blood drawn and then held up to the light to make sure it really exists, or a welling tick of blood spreading across a hot tongue. The stories Mr. Nobody tells Joey make his face even more hideous than it already is — make his nose hairs longer and spikier and more dewy with snot. Fevered with anger, Joey turns to the teapot and contemplates the temperature of the tea inside. It fills itself with blood and pours furiously out. A teapot cannot fill itself with blood and pouring is never furious — only a little grumpy. The whole class scratches out that line and then we move on to talk about finding our 'voice.' Under the bed or thereabouts. I've looked everywhere — please believe me — so I'm stuck with writing lines like: 'And when Mr. Nobody turned on the taps to soften his shaving brush, blood came tumbling after.' A clot on the brown paper. Vinegar in the wound. Virginia on the mount. A gunshot whistling softly past the waxy eardrum of an enemy ear.

Joey notices a new figure at the kitchen window. It is Dora peering in. It's a good thing that her children are all grown-up and living elsewhere. They would find it difficult to be reunited with a mother who they thought was dead and up the churchyard.

In the village pond a body shows up, bloated and bobbing, but it's the body of a rat and that happens.

Overhead, my grandfather, tucked up in the cold belly of a

plane fiddling nervously with his buttons, fills another gap in a story. This one. He was never meant to be a soldier, unlike Mr. Nobody who greedily licked the metal of his gun before shoving it inside her and blowing her insides out. He was never meant to see the cruelty of men, being the son of a minister and a good boy, so scared of going down pit that he ran off to war because he was sure it would be better to die above ground.

'My grandfather was a soldier, too,' says the director. 'It messed the whole family up.'

They come home and set up barracks inside their council houses, just to gain back all those lost years. He wanted to lie on his bunk and scale the mountains inside his head, but the 24-hour clock wouldn't let him. He wanted to float to the end of the universe just to discover that it was endless, but someone was shouting at him to polish his boots.

And then the blood. And then the women. And then the lies and the clap. And all the displaced persons and dirty refugee mouths. And then the strap of the rifle. Tin can. Tin ping. Hole in the chest. Convulsing friend, stay with us and come back to London, for Molly, for Molly. And the thin liquor, fought over. And then the selfish children and the even more selfish grandchildren ripping all the heads off your snap dragons, Grandad, so that you have to begin again. Always beginning again. After coming home, after scrapping the first plan to love Dora and the second to tolerate her, after seeing that no amount of soap was going to wash away the dirty waste of your life, that was war.

'Yeah, mine too,' I say.

# 30

Let's begin again.

A helicopter beds down on the lawn of More House with a freshly hired crew. The film will be shot over a period of two months. It is the story of a wealthy lord who resides in a mansion overlooking around-these-parts and the hamlet of More. In the surrounding fields at the right time of year, lambs do lamby things like springing on their springy legs and maa-ing with my uncle's fingers on their flopping gullets shaking the funny words out. Stop it!

The Lord is a well-known poet. Famous people pull up in carriages and stay for weeks at a time nursing nervous breakdowns and two weeks in the south would do you the world of good, but More House will have to suffice for now. There are shrill women and their rough mates. Lesbians in trousers. Rich gentlemen and what they have caught backstage. Dancers without escorts. The bitter sons and daughters of public figures. Poetesses. Painters. Opera singers.

---

The girl steps out of the house holding a rug. She drapes it over an iron railing — not in London and without Mrs. Dalloway spikes — and begins beating it. Through a cloud of dust she sees a carriage pulling up. It has dropped its entrails off at the front of the house and is now being driven to the stable by Solomon. 'Have those stable hands been here?' she thinks. 'On these breasts?' She puts down the rug beater and begins smoothing her hands over the front of the dress — up and down, getting lots of good ideas. The house has a front and a back. Like a human being.

The director suddenly cuts the scene. She cannot make up her mind which side of the house interests her and runs off around the front with her chair following close behind her. Nothing is happening. The rest of the cast and crew are dozing on the lawn, under bee traffic.

The girl goes off to the stables to find Solomon. He has been sleeping in her bed for a month now and has almost milked her dry. If it wasn't for him her milk would have already dried up and she wouldn't have to put folded cloths inside her bra to soak up the flow of milk that vainly tries to run down her belly and legs, over her feet, out of More House, over the fields, into the village, into the vicar's house, past the wife, up the stairs, into the baby's room, up the leg of the cot, and into the sleeping, slightly open mouth of Joey.

'What are you doing?' says the girl.

'Picking her hoofs,' says Solomon.

'Oh.'

'What are you doing?'

'Beating his rug.'

'Oh.'

'Are you sleeping in my bed tonight?'

'Can I?'

'You can, but you may not.'

'Huh?'

'Nothing.'

'Well, can I?'

'Sure.'

'Can I touch you?'

She shrugs. 'Sure.' The director is calling me. 'I have to go.'

'And ... ACTION!' The girl springs out of the house like a lamb. She is clutching a Persian rug, because after all the whole Turkish thing is always a delight. She lovingly drapes the rug of her love over an iron railing and it doesn't matter what kind because it is only a flipping railing get on with the story. As she beats her rage out on the innocent rug (rugs have no feelings) she is covered by a cloud of dust which causes her to cough like an old maid with pleurisy sputtering phlegm into the innocent hands (hands too) of the child who is always caught at the end of a game holding that asexual cat-cuddler. The child being me. Out of the corner of her eye she sees a cat with its paw about to come down on an innocent beetle. A little live creature. All creatures great and small can and do come towards the page bearing the tag INNOCENT.

The dust settles back to where is was first startled from, and the rug is dragged back inside and up to the master's master bedroom where the indent of his body has left the blankets and sheets kinky. The girl fills the mould of his body with plaster of Paris. Lets it set. Stands it up. Paints it pink. Glues on hairs she has gathered from plug holes and soap skins. Carves a hole between the hips. Straps on her leather penis and pushes it, pumps it into the hole, while she angrily smacks its deformed plaster buttocks. The awful sound of cracking as his crack splits and he falls in two directions — to either side of her leather erection — makes the sound technician blush with pride.

The dust settles. She is nowhere even close to revenge. That is my job, Joey's desire. Her job is to take the rug, now covered with plaster dust, back outside — in order to give it another good beating.

---

The love between Solomon and the girl is fluted. It has a ruffled, difficult shape — one that doesn't fit easily into this, or any narrative. Seeing as we're in this narrative, though, it is best to explain why it doesn't fit here.

Mostly it is that the girl, who has been betrayed before (in previous novels), seeks only more betrayal. When a young man comes into her life, with his butterfly-wing skin and his Lolita girlfriend waiting in some pink bedroom for him to come to her window, he is simply a distraction. There will always be bigger, fatter, more aggressive love to be siphoned from men like the Lord, and it will always be only a matter of time before that love knocks on her door at 3 in the morning and says, through the circle of a yawn: 'It's your turn. He said bring the dildo.' And the girl will tuck in the sleeping Solomon, kiss him on the forehead and tiptoe off to the Lord.

Why? Because his demands give her meaning. She follows the rootlets of scenes that have been pulled up, dripping earth, and thrown to the end of Dora's garden, looking for who she is. Her name. She follows her character smack into a coin being passed to a chemist, into the neat slip of a vial of poison into the pocket of a nurse, into her own back, bent by artificial rape, her breath savage, the cat INNOCENT. She follows these lines as best she can, trying to 'get it,' but little happens. And her prettiness is questionable. Her womb already used.

She cannot love Solomon because he loves her. The wound of rejection must gape. Always. Without the Lord's orders she is nothing. She is a character by association. And even with all my good intentions I cannot, at this moment, do anything to make her matter. It is up to her. She must decide how the pattern will run awry in the fingers of the rebellious embroiderer. She must make her footsteps heavier in order to wake up the whole house — all the workers, all the visitors, all the aborted and abandoned babies.

# 31

The girl's decision to rewrite the script is not up for negotiation. Her power overrides the director's power because the girl, as my protagonist, is primarily under contract to me (blood sister, ancestor, story line) and can, at any time, omit or create entirely new scenes, because I told her she could. The director has asked me to wield threats at the girl, but I have to keep telling her and her noisy crew that I've never written a novel or directed a film and don't know the rules. She thinks that's a lame excuse, but whatever she thinks doesn't matter. The girl is a rebel. Forthright and slightly looney. She gets knocked down, yes, but she knows how to get back up quickly and with the least amount of fuss. I've got to give it to her, she's a lot sturdier than most and deserves to have some say about what happens to her. After all, it's her life.

She has small hands, with fingers rough from spending too much time submerged in dishwater. At the bottom of the well is a dropped dead leaf. But that isn't here. In the wide slab of light is light. In the back corner of the stable is the absence of light. In the fire that crackles through a damp log is the voice of the storyteller. She has taken these few moments and spun a tiny web and in the centre she has placed a plastic spider. There is no web. There is no spider. She spins nothing, but watches water spin down the drain while she snatches carrot tops out of the circling wet. And then she tunes her hum into the song of his sneaking self that comes up all roses from the scullery behind.

The Lord has come to the kitchen in search of the girl. 'What are you doing?' he wants to ask, but instead he just stares at her. She is doing the vegetables. Hannah's orders. There is one pie left to fill and close. The rest are done. And here's one I prepared earlier. The set decorator will bring it out in a minute.

The Lord is wearing a dress that he has borrowed from Mary Shelley. Drunk and hairy-handed, he took it from her room during her last visit. It's a black dress — one she wore to Steven's funeral, which happened scarcely a day after her arrival. She liked the feel of his hand in hers as he helped her down from her carriage. Her legs were weak from sitting for so long and so she leaned into him, forcing out the muscles in his arm. To stay close to him for a little bit longer she invited him to share the umbrella he offered her.

The girl looks at the Lord and smiles. The sleeves of his dress are torn at the cuffs to fit his wolf hands, and two black silk stumps protrude from either shoulder. 'I love you,' he says. For a second she, I, you, believe him. The dress is proof of his devotion, as is the fact his voice is teetering on six-inch stiletto heels.

'I'm busy,' she says, turning back to the kitchen sink.

We wince and duck down into a codependent group hug.

He runs off to the garden to have a good cry, while the girl runs a carrot-wet hand down her bulge.

'Cut! What was that?' asks the director to the girl.

'What?'

'That stupid out-of-character bullshit you just pulled? And you,' she turns to the Lord, who is poking his head around the scullery door. 'Who told you to wear that dress?'

'The girl told me to,' he says, kind of pointing at her, but then thinking better of it and putting his hand back by his side.

'That would *never ever* happen in real life. We're going for authenticity here. We don't have a budget to cover anything but real life. We need fucking real fucking life!'

She walks off, her chair following behind her obediently, to find my brothers and sisters chasing each other in the copse. The wind in the treetops will soothe her, iron out her crinkles for the next scene. Well, that's what the girl thinks which must be what I think too.

## Aside

*Writers are liars. Good liars. We're like married men — telling you what you want to hear just to push one more line into you. We wear falsies — all types — and opt for plastic surgery when things start to hang a little heavily. And we'll do anything for a bit of attention — murder, rape, incest, torture. We'll beat someone to a pulp, and fuck someone in the ass, or whatever is necessary to get under the reader's eyebrows to push them up. Our favourite phrase is, 'Look at me!' which can be translated into Spanish as* 'Ámame!'

# 32

The girl is walking through the village wearing Solomon's Sunday best. The two are almost the same size, but it is obvious, around the shoulders especially, that the suit is not her own. She is not a smartly tailored lesbian — not yet, anyway — but more a sheep in wolf's clothing.

'Through' is the passing from one point to another with the points constantly shifting, receding, falling out of the viewfinder. Focus on the part where she turns slightly to watch the story being told again, as she turns slightly to watch the way a local boy's mouth opens and closes around a boast.

She turns as friction against a fraction of this story, as a line being crossed on the tottering ankles of a teenage girl twirling a sweaty daisy in her hand. Greening. On her way to a train station in another century and season. Her costume ripped from the pages of a sexual fantasy, she wears the traditional outfit of the woman who asked for it. 'Total crap,' she says. 'The only thing I'm asking for is a chance to transcend what I've been lumped with: this uncomfortable outfit, a boyfriend who has zits and doesn't wash properly, and a short future with a violent end.' She's tired of her cliché role. It won't let her blisters heal over.

'Good morning,' the girl says to the girl.

'Morning.'

The smiles they flatter each other with are not theirs to give, but have been stolen from a yet to be painted painting. Their smiles are broad and genuine. The director suddenly runs onto the scene shouting 'Cut!' but nobody is listening to her anymore, because I've told them not to. In a few pages she will probably tell them all not to listen to me.

The two girls even go so far as to stop in their lines in order to embrace each other. They hug for a long time and silence falls on the villagers and the crew. Some even bow their heads, a little ashamed for not having considered that everyone needs to be held from time to time — even characters, and especially characters with short futures and violent ends. After the embrace the girls are happy and secure and have high self-esteem.

'I like the bulge in your trousers,' says the one.

'I like the tightness of your miniskirt,' says the other.

Bessie, one of the Lord's horses, has escaped (Where's Solomon? Sleeping in the hay of America? Dozing down by the creek?) and is clattering through the village. It is good to watch the girl turn to see if this line is bringing up her rear logically, if this sentence is coming up against the ram of a period. Her turn is a pivot on which the story balances. Everything falls to either side of the pivot, the fold. The village shops hang on with their fingernails only. The runaway horse criss-crosses from paragraph to paragraph, galloping against the flow of potential traffic.

The girl, about to be trampled by the maniacal horse, tells the story to 'Stop!'

It flickers feebly and goes out.

After a few minutes of nervous anticipation, the light returns and directs its hymns at animal fur and bird feathers, because now, like then, like here, like now, rushing in are creatures from the highlands of a George MacDonald novel; all rising their dark blood heat through cracks in the road — not sure whether they are chasing or being chased. Tears stammer relief and joy down the girl's cheeks, as she watches animals and birds rush to their freedom. With her. She can see the embroiderer of this moment sitting on a chair in the middle of the road — letting stitches fall and get dragged off on the wind of fleeing creatures. Her thin, pretty hair lifted and lifting.

Bessie rears away from the girl, finds a patch of grass, and droops her head to graze. The girl is drawn to the rebellion, but has only two legs and no wings. She watches as the last sweating pelts of animal legs and noises run back to their own stories. Then she takes Bessie's halter and tugs at it. The horse snorts and obeys.

There is a look of terror on the dead girl's face. Her daisy has had the green squeezed out of it and droops like the head of a horse.

'Don't worry,' says the girl to the girl. 'Sometimes a person's unconscious is split and let loose at the world. The contents are mostly four-footed or on wings. But that was nothing. It's when crustaceans and plankton and electric eels work their way to the surface that you know you've hit your shadow side straight on the temple.'

'Whose unconscious was that?' asks the girl, plucking her knickers from her crack.

'Yours, I think.'

---

The hems of the girl's trousers swish deliciously through the tall meadow grass. It's about the route she takes home from the village, her usual way. Through the foxy pasture and past the basking sows. Down the sun-cutting path and over the mended sty. It's the line of the journey and the fact that the fox comes before the pig comes before the trail comes before the sty. Without knowing the order, the whole journey circles endlessly, swallowing its own tail and then spitting it out a thudding line. The line of the story can't handle the nagging details of the sagging in-between. That's my job — to handle, to put up with, to fill gaps with soldiers.

She comes humming down the long field, stopping here and there to let the horse eat. The water trough is a graveyard for grass flecks and insects and the field rises up a shaken blanket to meet the fringe of a wood. Foxes hide and foxes sleep, but occasionally one crosses a day-lit field, stops abruptly and turns his head directly at you. He says, 'I am a dog, but you cannot walk me.' He says, 'I will eat your hens later on tonight.'

Letting Bessie free — with a little slap to her flank — she climbs over the gate. If you zoom the camera to her left you will see her turn slightly to follow a story move out of the corner of her eye. It is the Lord, at the bottom of the field holding up a large banner that says in thick red paint I LOVE YOU. In the pocket of his dress is a poem that he will later write. For now, his hands are busy holding taut his confession. Only she can't be bothered to look (It's her prerogative now, not mine), and jumps down from the gate in her suited boy-body, turning her head in a different direction — at Holly, in with the chickens, making the traditional clucks and tuts.

# 33

The Lord turns thirty-eight at his own party. Guests come from all over England and other nooks and crannies of Europe to gorge and lust and fuck.

Long into the night the house is a private noise leaking into the village. Music skims over the gravestones in the churchyard, stops a fox in his usually silent tracks, drives a poacher even deeper into necessity. By 5 AM the house is just the breath of sleepers. The painted are breathing. The painter is sleeping off his gluttony. Poems are spilling from empty glasses, crying, 'Who's going to write us?'

But in one room in the house there is no sleep. The girl sits at the end of her bed, facing a wardrobe mirror. She looks at her face for so long that she sees a stranger there, a ghoul, a looking witch.

The mirror's surface is a wall between desire and its fulfilment. Everything is fixed in the details with a screwdriver and that gorgeous look of concentration right there in a line across her face. At the core is the matter at hand. Shreds of god release into lightening sky a scattering of birds, of pages, which throws us off the fate of this story. Press on and be brave. Kiss the mirror. The tongue will fold uselessly against the cold glass, but at least it's a start.

Something tender is about to happen. The house is a sleeping kingdom, about to be disturbed by one hell of a charming prince. He comes in peace with his palms open, facing up at a thorny thicket that thins and comes away in his hands, sending bats upward into doves, night into day. The forest bows to listen to the message of this strange man. He brings a message that is so tender it must come in the form of a kiss.

The kingdom is sleeping, but for the girl. This surprises the prince considerably, who thought his kiss was capital and that his prize would be waiting flaccid and bad-breathed for him to pick up like dry cleaning. He checks his map and his instructions, while the girl continues kissing and licking her reflection, oblivious to his beauty refracting its radioactive hum off her mirror.

'Are you Sleeping Beauty?'

The girl turns. She sees the prince for the first time. Solomon — wearing an outfit borrowed from Adam Ant. 'Well, what do you think?'

'No.'

'Good guess.'

There is a long pause. The girl gets up from her bed and goes to the window. The lawns are panting down into the holes of worms. Everything is alive and reeking of alcohol. A lactating spasm of dawn light makes a futile attempt to rouse the girl's romantic instinct, but she is bored shitless of princes and lords and grooms and vicars and fathers. She is tired of being mistaken for someone who actually cares. It is now so late that we call it early; she is exhausted and there is some goddamned poser in her room, pretending that one of his kisses can restore her to life even though she is already very much alive.

'You're delusional.'

'Why?'

'Because a prince doesn't need to do so much work just to get some.'

'True.'

'So why don't you just head on home.'

---

It is five in the morning when my parents find me sleepwalking out of the house with a small red suitcase and a script. As they come closer they can see a tiny prince caught between my teeth. His heart has been punctured and a thin trickle of his blood has stained one of my lower incisors.

Houses are dangerous holes of irrationality, which is the reason I'm leaving. Anything can happen inside a house, but letting the outside world know that something is happening inside the house is virtually impossible. Children wave flags from windows, drop tightly folded SOS notes into the shoes of visiting aunties, draw pictures in Art class of Daddy doing bad things to Mummy, write stories in English class about things children shouldn't know. But all these messages get eaten by the birds of the forest. Hungry birds. Greedy birds, ruining everything with their sinful gluttony. Don't their dirty little sparrow brains know what is at stake? What they are messing with for the sake of a crumb or two?

The problem with houses is that their doors have hinges and handles. It is easy to hear somebody coming. When feet touch the floor, even if it is carpeted, it creates a sound that says, 'Stop.' And he always does.

Once I reach the main road — so main it is called London Road and once went all the way there — my mother decides it is time to intervene.

'The answer,' she says, 'is inside you.'

I swallow the dead prince and stick out my thumb. It is time to leave home. I am nearly nine years old, for chrissake! Her special clichés do nothing to appease me. I put my hand into my gut and palpate the wet stuff I find there, searching for 'the answer'. The gesture is flippant and, for me, comical. The proof lies in the pudding of my guts — my tasty, sloppy guts, where the answer is obviously nowhere to be found. My mother, paralyzed by my gory performance, lets me get into a van that has just pulled up to the curb of my thumb. It is full of drunken men — including the driver — who say they are looking for a bit of pussy. 'That'll be me,' I say, and climb in.

*If the answer is inside me then why has only one prince who can thin a thicket with just his fingers been sent down to tell me that? I want to listen to him speak. I want to hear the Lord. The people in the kingdom come to hear him speak and they see that he is good. And so it is written. Written here.*

I have a prim chin and an attitude that I'd slap the shit out of now because it isn't child abuse when it's on the face of your own eight-year-old self. Cockiness is cheap. An inexperienced gob attempting to smack the propriety out of a person who's already been there and done that. I slap the girl across the face. I tell her that next time she tells the Messiah to 'head on home' she'll be really sorry. Her response is to say, 'How sorry? This sorry?' holding her thumb and index finger a few inches apart.

---

With Prince Charming now vanquished, Solomon sees his chance. At the bottom of the stairs (Granny's slippery ones) he strips off down to boots, suspenders and long johns, leaving his frills and gimmicks in a pile for the costume designer to pick up. When the girl reaches the bottom of the stairs Solomon brings out his finest Charles Dickens arc, rounding her off with a flourish of brass.

But it is difficult to catch the girl's attention so early in the morning, when the air sags under the weight of another lark rising. She merely brushes past him, suspecting that he is a moth that has lost its way to the moon. Her thoughts are elsewhere, on the tug in her womb, the helix spinning a mouth and anus on the choppy waves of nausea; on the basket of apples she is carrying — fat and crisp and ready to break their waters onto the remnants of last night's madness.

A woman is asleep in an alcove on the landing, like a pile of vomit, a pile of coats and hats, a half-eaten piece of bread, of cheese, the corpse of a wine glass in a pool of its own blood. The girl passes. The apples pass. Solomon passes the girl with her womb full of apples and her apples memorizing the rootlets of trees. A stork hangs its burden on a tree in the orchard and the tree's branches curl around the mewing burden.

The girl, suddenly lit up from behind by a heavenly light that seems to burst from the mouths of hymns, lowers her eyes with a modesty that would touch the heart of any good pervert, which tells us that she is in the presence of the Lord. He has stumbled out of the dining room and is made up of three parts — head, thorax and abdomen — and sporting a grotesque mane of vomit-matted hair. His heart is touched when he sees the girl and he comes towards her through the fug of his morning breath, letting out a fart that he tries to keep in, but that is too quick for him. Solomon hears this and spins back around on the smooth cobbles of his master plan.

'Leave her alone!'

The Lord looks over the girl's shoulder at the skinny, half-dressed boy standing behind her who he recognizes to be one of his grooms.

'Excuse me?'

'I said, leave her alone!'

The girl turns on Solomon's pathetic attempt to turn her into a damsel and mutilates his self-esteem with one look.

'I love you!' he shouts, as he runs out of the house to the sound of gravel against boot. My favourite.

The Lord looks at the girl. 'What was that?' he asks.

'Love.'

'Hmm.'

'I have something to tell you.'

'Uh-huh?'

'I have vomited every morning this week.'

'Get rid of it.'

The girl takes the basket of apples to the set decorator, who fusses over her and tells her not to lift such heavy things while she is pregnant. She then goes to see Hannah, who brews her some special tea, which the girl takes to her room to drink. Wanting to be alone, she is annoyed to find the dead girl sitting on her bed; sitting there looking like she knows what it's all about with her bleached hair and lipstick lips. She has taken the girl's strap-on out from under the bed and is threatening to throw it out of the window if she comes any closer.

'You wouldn't dare!' shouts the girl.

'Wanna bet!?' screams the other, lobbing the stitched phallus out into the garden. 'Women like you make it harder for the rest of us!'

Us?

It lands in a passing wheelbarrow, pushed by a half-blind gardener who, after hearing a thunk, roots around in his cargo of firewood. Feeling nothing out of the ordinariness of wood, he continues to the back of the garden. Less than an hour later the girl's penis dies in a bonfire.

The girl runs downstairs and out of the house where she performs a search and rescue operation that is in vain. Her dew soaked fingers (probably) rip the heads (or tails?) off worms in her searching rage. The male and female parts of flowers (probably) bend and wet and powder her hands. She smells of the funky exploration of childhood.

After the girl has given up searching and gone back into the house, the garden gets back to work. It works hard, like a Quaker. It brings up life and then it lets it down.

# 34

Mrs. Nobody gets fished out of a polluted river. Her heart has mutated, but is suited well to the climate of her marriage with Mr. Nobody. Occasionally she considers the life she could have had, but never for long because it is too painful. Her husband, being the breadwinner, quickly becomes more important to her than her son. Such logic could only exist within a capitalist society within which she has always lived. But worse. Born poor and raised to believe that money forms a warm blanket that smothers the life out of misery, that suffocates the pain of hunger and want, she cannot help but stand firm in the wake of her husband's cruelty. She wanted the sugar. She wanted to lick it. She wanted a house with net curtains.

---

Joey touches the sequins on the dress of a photograph and then reaches for the scissors. Another fishy woman flickers to the floor of his bedroom. He gathers her up into an armful of arts and crafts materials and takes her over to the desk. Then he presses his cheek to the windowpane and stares at the condensation on the chipped sill. The scene is mundane, which means that the quiet crest of disaster is about to break. It comes in the form of a stepfather, which makes this a fairy tale.

Mr. Nobody is upstairs on the landing outside Joey's room, about to knock. I'll give him one point for that. Yes. One out of a hundred.

'Come in.'

'It's your mother's birthday. What have you got for her?'

Large and dangerous and certain silence.

'Nothing.'

Mr. Nobody enters, a bird with a broad wingspan and you'll get your mum something if I have to drag you down to the shops by your hair. Hairs. A whole clump of them loved by the fingers of fury. The clattering body of a boy dragged downstairs by his hairs. A whole clump of them. The window is wide open and has always had a way with Joey.

'I'll make her something.'

---

Mrs. Nobody is sitting in the living room watching television. Close by is a bowl of salted peanuts on a small table designed specifically for things like bowls of peanuts, reading glasses, folded newspapers, and a glass of lager of an evening never did anyone any harm. She can hear the sound of the peanuts being ground into butter between her teeth and it makes her feel hollow. Her hands are placed together in her lap like someone pathetic who has nothing better to do on her birthday than watch television. So she moves them, but it just feels more awkward and so she moves them back. Her husband. Her living room. Her two feet in their two slippers with their two corns, one on either big toe, almost covered by a long polyester dressing gown with cornflowers on it. My favourite flower, which shows some sympathy on my part for her loneliness and lack of style.

Happy Birthday Mum! is a picture passing into her hands made of smaller pictures cut out from a magazine.

'Oh, lovey, it's beautiful! Joey, that's so thoughtful of you, love. Why don't you put it on the mantlepiece for everyone to see. Look at what Joey's made for his mam.'

Suddenly we're back in Yorkshire and that's not a problem because even that far north there are magazines and bowls of peanuts and polyester dressing gowns. And Dora is at the window trying to get in out of the rain, but she has been drawn out by curtains, and of course, cancer. Her face is dribbling with rain but she remains there in her zombie splendour.

Mr. Nobody is wearing a belt. He stands behind the couch looking over his wife's shoulder at her present, letting the cut-outs of fashion models prancing in heels across their new cardboard home sink into his mind. At the centre of the collage is Joey's head cut out from a photograph of his body. The head is balancing on the elegant neck of a supermodel who is wearing a green sequined dress. On her feet are green, sparkling stilettos. On her hands are gloves that run lovingly almost to the elbow. Also green. Joey's face in the photograph is smug like he thinks it's a joke that he is making his stepfather look like a laughingstock.

'You want to be a girl, huh? You think you're a bloody girl? When I was a lad we'd have called your sort a fairy and I bet things haven't changed that much since then. Why'd you have to go and upset your mother on her birthday? Why'd you want to embarrass her like this?'

And even though Joey's mother is making objections either to being upset or embarrassed she does so in the kind of birdlike voice that the wives of violent husbands eventually acquire and is not even prepared to attempt to wrestle the picture out of Mr. Nobody's hand as he marches to the fire, his face burning, tearing the picture in half and placing it in the fire like so. Zoom in on the picture being licked by flames, and curling and browning at the edges. A typical shot.

'You're not a bloody girl and do you know why? Do you know why, you bloody selfish bastard?!'

Mr. Nobody has the floppy, passive Joey by the waistband of his trousers and is almost lifting him off the floor as he struggles to pull down the little boy's fly.

'Because of this. This! This is why you're not a fucking girl!'

Mr. Nobody is holding between his thumb and forefinger the eight-year-old penis of his stepson. He is wiggling it about to emphasize his point. Mrs. Nobody has covered her eyes with her hands and is sobbing. The picture has been completely consumed in the fire. The model never got to keep the dress, as Joey imagined she would. She went home after the photo shoot and ate a sandwich that she bought at a café on the walk home. The sandwich was wrapped in cling film so its contents were visible. When she got to her apartment she unwrapped the sandwich and sat down at the kitchen table to eat it. The sound of her mouth chewing made her sad.

Dora can hear what is happening. She rattles against the window pane an angry wind. All to get out of the rain. Mr. Nobody lets the thing drop and goes off. Joey zips himself up and goes back upstairs to his room. He pulls a piece of orange peel out from the weird stash under his bed and sucks on it. The scissors are still out on the floor. He puts them into the drawer of his desk and flops face down onto his bed. When Mrs. Nobody comes upstairs Joey is sleeping on top of his quilt, with the light still on, which is a waste of electricity.

# 35

I wear my darkest eyes to the theatre. During the film I stand up and turn around and look at the faces of the people who have come, like me, to watch this movie. The faces in all the rows look at me instead of the movie, until in a rain of popcorn and insults I sit back down and continue watching the film.

It's a film about us.

The first thing there has to be is a first thing. First things first. There is a writing time limit of one hour, which tonight I am breaking in order to travel back to an event that I want to unwrite, reconfigure.

I go into the living room at London Road just to see if my stepfather is still there, sitting on the couch smoking a fag and watching the news.

'Sit down. You're in my way,' he says.

I sit next to him and lean over slowly until my ear is on his stomach. It gurgles a demonic language. 'Gog and Magog. Gog and Magog.' My angelic eight-year-old cheek rests on his belt buckle. I hear the voice of the news anchorman competing with the sounds coming from the fireplace, from the rain outside, from the gurgling stomach.

The woods and their stained mattresses are far away, but domesticated girls curl like cats on men's crotches all over this town. We are privileged to the softest finger-streams running all over our hair. Our hairs. Gently does it.

Fish is a game he has invented. Under the sound of open taps his cooing voice quivers. He smiles so that my sister and I think that his playing around with our vaginas is a fun game.

'Here comes the swishy fishy.'

Its fins never touch us. It's the water that's doing all the work as the flickering of the fish's finger-tail sends underwater waves over our slits. Fishy takes the long way around the bathtub so as not to seem obvious. Girling. It gets done. My mother is on the phone with her friend. They get through a bottle of wine-stained glasses, while their daughters come undone at all the wrong places.

Suddenly my sister stands up in the bath. Water roars down her. She is Niagara Falls in miniature. The soldier shape of her six-year-old body salutes the general of her meaning, with a 'Yes, Sir. At your service, Sir!' She means something to me. She means something to herself. And she has something important to say.

'What are you doing, Dad?'

'Playing.'

'What's that in your trousers? It's always there during the fishy game. What is it? I want to see it. Show it to me.'

I'm rooting for her. Still in my water blanket, but with an imaginary bucket of popcorn in my hands. 'Yeah, we want to see what that is,' I say. 'Show us!'

Make us a film. Make us a show. Prance before us in your gay-public-schoolboy Milton paper dress. Plant your dirty Morris-dancing tin-whistle in our vaginas. Show us the ribbons of our sister's maypole madness in the rotten cave of your crotch. You can have an erection. We give you permission. My sister's body is a perfected present from the gods, and they were erect when they made her and popped her into your greedy mouth. They make her out of marble and they paint her pink and put her into a house that has doors that close tragically behind her and us and our mother, who is downstairs talking blah-blah-blah on the telephone, drinking glass after glass of wine to numb the pain of marrying you.

You've got us where you want us and you say, 'Here comes

the little fishy!' And it goes from her coral reef to mine via a warm current of pee. The yellow, concealed under the bubbles, warms my back with its sunny joy, reminding me that my sister is there in the bath behind me, going through this experience too. I know that we will be women one day and we will sit down at a kitchen table with a nice cup of tea and we will ask each other if that 'game' you played was appropriate or inappropriate and we will both vote for inappropriate.

I stand her up in the bathtub of my novel because she was always so tough and soldier-like and she looks you in the eye and tells you to get out of the bathroom so that we can continue playing Cake Shop in peace and you leave the bathroom to the sound of her saying, 'Will that be two bubble cakes or three, Mrs. Smith?' 'Make it three, please. And throw in a couple of soap pies, while you're at it.' 'OK. That'll be 50P, please.'

---

Why have I come looking for my stepfather? Each of his eyes contains a miniature Doberman Pinscher. They charge out from the snowy field to warn me, are dragged back, then charge out at me again. I gather my fingers together and hold them in front of my throat. You do not do. You do not do.

His idea is rotten. He buries his head. He has taken his shirt. He is answering. He does everything. His mouth is burning. He touches the pepper. His fingers are burning. He is not afraid to ask. He is being answered. He is alive.

When I enter the room he has gone. The place where he was sitting is still warm. I touch it. The television is off so I can now hear Dora rapping to get in. I draw the curtains and open the glass patio door. She steps over the threshold between death and life, albeit fictional, and takes a seat close to the fire. She is dying and she is dead. The punctum of the photograph is the hole in her stocking that she vainly stretches the hem of her skirt to conceal. From that hole many stories are told. The one about the briar that caught it. The one about the word that scolded it. The one about the day she went to her sister's to pick up the package he had sent her from Yorkshire that contained stockings.

She asks me where he's gone. 'Perhaps to the dogs?' I say. They've been waiting for him in the alley behind our house — his own dream killer-dogs — and they slobber violently at the thought of his liver and onions. She sees that my hand continues to hover over the place he'd been sitting, and silently wishes she could meet me under different circumstances. But I need her morphine wings. I need her dangerously-sharp-cheekbones photograph.

His Dobermans cannot protect him from the wrath of a dead grandmother, snuck into his house by a clever granddaughter who refuses to keep the secret ticking time on her inherited crazy clock.

She wants to tell him that she is watching him. But he has gone. He will eventually kill himself. And Dora and I will be there. With popcorn.

Dora tells me about the night she left the orphanage. It was summer. Her son cried. He raged like a crazed monkey, tried to wriggle out of the arms of one of the volunteers, because he knew what was happening to him. My grandfather met her at the gate and said, 'It's for the best,' then gave her four more babies and a box of chocolates to replace her son.

Dora tells me that she remembers the sound of her heels taking her in a direction that her body didn't want to go. Away. Stretching the umbilical cord so far it snapped and floated away a gossamer thread plucked from the leaf of a poetry book. At home she ran a bath and sat in it. She sat and she waited for something to happen. She held her knees in her arms and rocked back and forth.

And then the place where his head pushed out into the world rotted. It turned in upon itself, eating Dora alive. It cried for the boy to come back, sealing down angrily over my grandfather's needs, pushing him farther into his pint, into the glint of other women's lips.

And then she died.

And then her replacement came to the house wearing rubber gloves and a lot of lipstick. She worked at a canteen from Monday to Friday, washing the dishes of grammar school boys who played rugby and got drunk and fucked secondary school girls on the weekends. The rest of the time she worked for my Grandad.

And there he is, slightly off-set. Half here. Half not. The sergeant-major of housework, desperate to reach down and wipe away a single speck of dust from his left boot but scared to move a muscle. We film him while he makes her hoover, while he hovers around her, pacing, checking, organizing, lost in the details of his mental checklist, having to begin again, begin again. What was she supposed to do today? What was it? What was it? The silverware?

Two women rot before his very eyes and they know he is the reason for their decay and he knows it too and every time they look at him they see the streak of hatred that lives in his teeth and in his Aryan eyes. Nothing makes sense. He has the pipe and the cap and the Jack Russell of everyone's fantasy grandad, so why does he have the ability to suck the opera from the lungs of one wife, the wheezy laugh from the chest of the other? When they die, he takes the remnants of their lives — the smell of their clothes, the sound of their makeup bags, the puff of their talcum powder — and bins the lot. I come looking for a keepsake in the drawers that they once touched, but except for a few photographs, which have no smell, I find nothing. I worry that they are both figments of my imagination. Grandmothers from space.

---

When Grandad found out about the fishy hands of my stepfather he got on a train and went down the bay, where there was plenty of sea cabbage and a lot of litter washed up from the channel ferries, and he took a walk. But that wasn't what he did. He never went anywhere alone. He cried and saw in the mirror that tears were cutting into his shaving foamed face. Then he watched golf on television. But he didn't do that either. I don't know how long he sat on the edge of the bed looking straight ahead at the wardrobe, but when he finally came downstairs his knees were stiff. He turned off the landing light, cheap dark, before coming downstairs, and as he homed in on the sound of horse racing it crossed his mind.

> *He said that the boy had to go and when he said that he broke the women in his family from the men and they have remained, to this day, broken. And so it is written. Written here.*

# 36

The girl comes back to me. She has a wailing christening with breath. I huff her dried fig with life and when I open it each seed is a word from the Bible. Always there is somebody who knows better answers, leaving us with a feeling of inadequacy. Everything we do is wrong and everything the shepherd does is right. His crook digs into the girl's neck and hurts her. She carries the story of Cain, who watched his brother's blood meander through the dust, desperate to relocate the circular trail of all living things, but pushed back by the dust to live in lines. Desperate. Pushed back. Desperate. Pushed back. The blood meandered all the way through Genesis and beyond and everyone lived for hundreds of years, turned into clay and were breathed on and made flesh once more.

She comes back with her hair loose and her face flushed by the foetus inside her. She is not delighted by the Turkish rug coming out from its place. The house is never finished. It is simultaneously being erected and dismantled. It crumbles into the tea. Soft. Sketched plans, rolled and poking from a pocket, never get off the ground; never get born and raised. Kept down by circumstance, the fastest way out of her fate is through the end of a movie. This one.

She'll be fine.

---

Arriving through the scullery door, she reaches immediately for an apron and puts it on. I don't ask her where she's been.

I'm not her mother. Finding there are no potatoes this week, she remembers that the crop has been pestered to death. The heavy mantle of global warming settles on her shoulders. She groans, curling her mind into a lunatic ball and letting it rock the locusts back and forth.

Until I remind her of positive thinking!

There are no potatoes, but there are plenty of carrots. A comfort. Focus on what you have, not what you don't, and just repress all the creepy crawly style thoughts.

Out in the garden her fingers touch the tendrils of those green-haired orange men, plucked from soil that may have been touched by druids and/or moles. Like the walk from More House to the village, the vegetable garden is a refuge from labour. Let out of the house for an hour to gather and tend vegetables and herbs is a delight. Her mouth fills with the same sunlight that makes its stake on the raspberries and peas. Coming and saying things about storms. That they come. That they shake up the placidity of the garden. That the wind makes the words come. And when they cannot be coaxed up the throat, I'm here to give them to you, as well as a raspberry and a pea *ad infinitum* until stomach ache sets in. The garden feeds the darling starlings. You. And me.

Joey is coming. He needs to hold his shoulders back. I keep forgetting to remind him. He passes here. Soon. The thing about Joey is the boiled sweet of anger that has gotten stuck in his throat. Its roots are gnawed by many rabbits but they never snap. Let him speak. He lines up behind his mother and waits. The best part of his tongue is the part that knows the taste of the raspberry. He gathers fruit in his T-shirt. And the girl eats it.

I cannot keep the family straight. The girl has no features. She puts her hand to her face and feels nothing but a smooth surface. Missing everything that should have been considered by the director and her crew. Or most probably by me. She's too much about skirt. Her skirt swishes and raises and is smoothed by worked hands. Her skirt is washed and hung black beside its white apron. I cannot keep my family out. In my mother's knickers drawer is a maid's outfit. She tells me to wear it to the Halloween party. When I arrive my friend's dad says, 'You look tasty.' Of course I do! I am a thirteen-year-old in a French maid's outfit that my parents ordered from the back of a wank mag and I'm dancing right beside his armchair to my favourite *Top of the Pops* song! He gets so excited that he drops a bowl of cheese and onion crisps on his hard on.

And here are the girl and Joey in the Lord's garden with no idea how they got there or why and I'm up in the sky with my ego puffed out like a blowfish. He runs his hand through his hair and then 'shuffles' out of the raspberry nets. She cuts open a 'pomegranate' and then 'sidles' over to him with her fruit-stained lips. The garden is lush. Everything is ripe and ready for picking and that, I suppose, is why they've come. There's enough mood. And light. Enough room in the basket. Enough urchins and beggars with sores in their mouths from missed nutrients calling to them over the fence. Enough reason to meet and discuss the plan. To draw it. To scale it. To cross it. To let it. To press on, even after dark, and without rations.

Joey and the girl sit on the warm, dry earth with their legs crossed and their eyes scanning over these dim lands of peas. They face each other, with a basket placed between them. Joey feeds his mother the contents of a swollen pea pod. He cares that she gets the finest foods at the lowest prices—never mind global warming. Then he opens his hand out. For she feeds there. And as she does so he strokes the back of her head.

'There, there,' he says.

'CUT!' shouts the director. 'I like this scene. Is it one of mine or one of yours?'

'I'm not sure,' I say. 'I think we can pretty much just stop even trying to separate things.' Everything's in the pond now, swirling into the sucking hole.

'I'm a little bit confused, though, as to what the scene has to do with the general arc of the story?'

I wish she would stop being a graduate student. Just for one second. It would help to remember that once upon a time a story was just a story, with a beginning, a middle, and an end, that temporarily wobbled but that always righted itself eventually.

'Well, I suppose this is where we enact a role reversal between Joey and his mother. Even though she in effect *abandoned* him, he still attempts to demonstrate that *despite* being always already in a state of problematic inertia, he has the insight *not* to capitalize on it?'

'Yes, I suppose you're right. Let's shoot it again but this time we'll have Joey holding his mother in his arms, like a baby.'

For this, we must shrink her. To the size of a doll.

# 37

Hannah lifts up the rolling pin and waves it at the others, laughing flour. This is what she'll do if her husband isn't careful and it's bigger and better than his. *Laughter.*

Enough! There needs to be a serious conversation between Hannah and the girl. It isn't funny that there needs to be, for once, someone who'll take things seriously around here. The other maids drop their heads and move off to either side of the set. The music is melancholy and slow. At the door one of the maids turns briefly to face the audience, but then looks down again. 'And . . . CUT!' The party is over girls. Clear the kitchen. Dim the lights. Let's have one candle placed between Hannah and the girl.

Hannah is fat and that's the only adjective she gets.

The girl is wearing the French maid's outfit from my mother's knickers drawer.

'What are you plotting?' she says, taking one of the girl's hands and sandwiching it between her own, a caught fish.

'I've got ideas. Lots of them. Joey's been giving them to me,' the girl says.

'Joey who?'

'Joey my son Joey.'

Hannah knows that the girl doesn't have a son, unless she counts the moments between her cunt and the woman from the orphanage, which, Hannah supposes, is probably what the girl is doing, being the queen of melodrama that she is.

'Interesting,' Hannah says.

The girl feels uncomfortable. She wants to pull her hand

away, but doesn't want to offend Hannah, who has now sensed this, has now read this, and lets the girl's fishy fingers swim away. It takes a moment for the girl to pull her hand back to the safety of her apron pocket. She doesn't like being touched in anything but a sexual way. Intimate touch is hot oil poured over an enemy — herself.

'Damn! I forgot to call the knife sharpener!' Hannah says, slapping the table. 'Do you know what happens to the babies from the orphanage? They get farmed out to the local farmers as workers. The vegetables and meat that the Lord eats, and the milk he drinks are products of his children's labour. Children for miles around have dark, curly hair. It is said that some even write poetry.'

'What's your point, Hannah?'

'Nothing. It's just interesting, that's all.'

'Not really,' says the girl. 'Have you ever had a baby taken from you — at birth, before you even get to hold it and feed it — which is then raised only to be used as cheap labour?'

'Yes,' says Hannah. 'Yes. Ever met the Lord's father who art in heaven, hallowed be his name?'

'Thy will be done, on earth as it is in heaven?'

'Forgive us each day our daily trespasses.'

'As we forgive those that trespass against us? It's all making sense now. The cord must be cut. Where are the blind mice? Where is the knife sharpener? Call him, Hannah, call him in!'

'That's not necessary, love,' says Hannah. 'I can help you.' Lean her forward and zoom in on her face, lit up in horror flick fashion. 'If you want my help, I can help you. I've had some ideas of my own, you know.'

'I don't need your witchcraft, Hannah. I just need your support.'

'Well, aren't you a poppet,' says Hannah, leaning forward to the pull of her wheezing bosom to pop a kiss onto the girl's forehead. 'You're almost a daughter to me. There, there.' She takes the girl's hand for a second time — this time a hand that meets hers halfway across the table. 'It's all going to be alright, my pet.'

There is nothing else to say, Hannah knows, but she continues to fuss, making hushing sounds and patting the girl's hand gently.

The girl's idea, which for now she is borrowing from Joey's Plot Shop, is to gather orphans like hazelnuts, bring them to More, and present them to the Lord on his birthday. There will be a midwife bringing out a live-on-TV baby, and others, gathered by Joey, sticking close to their brother. A whole bushel of siblings. Geese giving their feathers. Sheep giving their wool. Cows giving up their udders to be fumbled by famished babes.

The Lord, upon hearing where this story is heading, goes to Granny's room to sulk. When Grace knocks on the door to give him the news that Lord and Lady so-and-so cannot attend his dinner party he lobs a pillow at her in the name of the Lord 'Jesus Christ! Can't you see I'm busy plotting!'

At least somebody is.

The girl has already left to gather up the Lord's children. He will have to hire a cobbler to shoe them all, a tailor to don them all, a baker to feed them all. Bread will be broken and fish will come tumbling from baskets in silver lines.

'But who will play these extra children?' asks someone from casting. 'We only have enough money in our budget for three extras — and they're all adults.'

'This is a novel,' I say. 'Stop interrupting the flow of the line. Look. If you need lots of children just make them out of cardboard. Or just don't worry about it. What the hell am I supposed to do with a load of children anyway? Have a parade? And anyway, cardboard ones can't run around and mess everything up and I don't think real children are allowed to be on-set when a porno is being shot, are they? So just forget that last scene. Chalk it up to the girl's melodrama and just move along.'

I go to my trailer. I need to smoke cigarettes.

# 38

The girl's bed is just a stone's throw away from Grace's. They must be careful when throwing the stone, however, in case it hits one of the other sleeping girls. The main thing is that crossed rivers dry up and become beds. When she reaches the other side, Grace asks for her stone back before disappearing under the blanket with her hot, moonlit tendrils.

The girl, hanging her hand over the side of her bed, says, 'The first rule of divination is love your stick.' But from under the bed comes the frustrating reminder that the dead woman has ruined everything. That giant phallus, that when strapped into place made it impossible to get a word in edgewise, has gone.

The story must go on though, so the girl pulls the blanket away and sucks at Grace's nipple, rolls it in her saliva lick, arching her friend's back away from her hands that hold it together, thin and young bamboo. From vowel to consonant. Over. Again. Vowel consonant vowel vowel. Weakening each other's concentration. The day sliding off like something wet, slick, leaving them alone, shining somewhere under their bent heads of hair. Slow. Determined. Final.

'How was that?' says the girl, turning to the camera, wiping her mouth with the back of her hand.

But there is nobody there. The crew have all gone home for the night and it is only her and Grace making a scene out of nothing but the convenience of being horny and in the same room at the same time. It wasn't meant to happen now, but no worries — we can shoot the scene again later.

Hardly had the girl begun to rub her tired feet together,

when Grace came looking. Before she could say anything but yes, their legs and mouths and bellies were lifting up out of their nightdresses. For if the scene has to happen, whether we are all busy sleeping or relieving ourselves of lovers or urine, it will happen, in any bed, at any time. Covers will lift to reveal pages upon pages of pleasure. We will climb in and press against the body of our lover, eagerly, tender with relief. Our bodies will arch to the touch, sink down into the warm belly of forgetting, of abandon and warmth, the sweat and the lick, the raw rubbing open of the closed places that we have guarded safe from strangers. Bare. Before sunrise. Before the first note from the first bird quivers over the congregation, we will let go. With or without a director.

---

I sent my mother a copy of *The Lover* by Marguerite Duras because I wanted her to know that I was one. I wrote a message on the inside cover: *Is Freud at the house yet? Because if he is, I'm not coming.*

I don't want him to see and then take note. I don't want him to think that there is a rat chewing its way up my asshole and into my intestines while he sits there with his fingers in his beard and the previous patient's more interesting dreamscape occupying his mind.

'I'm paying a lot of money, Dr. Freud. Why can't you stay focused on me? Am I only interesting when I have a cigar in my mouth? Or when I tell you about the time I went upstairs in a house in which I was a guest just to finger myself on the toilet?'

Words. Sticks and stones. When the girl figures out that I'm just a stone's throw away, she'll smash my window. Then the wind will make a mainline to my stationary body and I'll be a bed that she'll make in the morning like tea. After all, only she can bleed me, Halal-style, of all my repressed sexual clots.

The doctor wants a narrative and he wants me to be touched in it. Inappropriately. I'm trying. I run from house to house looking for that Sunday afternoon lull, that inevitable come-down from a sugar high into the pool of his trousers, fingers, whispered crinkle-cut threats.

'There,' he says. 'Right there where Joey meets the girl outside the butcher's, is the place I want you to start.'

Trip. Get up. Trip. Get up. I grab my sister's hand. I am her safety net. With me she looks like she is wearing a veil, is hidden from all eyes. Occasionally I peek under the net and grin at her. We run our hands over the wobbling privet hedge, through the scent of nostalgia, of pre-summer, of evenings free to run in the lanes with our dog. Free too. Shitting in people's gardens. Springing up against my screeching at the fragile hips of old women. I control that animal. I hold her jaw together with my strong hand. Whip her with a negligible willow strand. She jumps again. Free. Happy.

The place he wants me to start at is a good one. There's nothing here to cry about, except perhaps the crow that is pecking at my sister's net, trying to get at her eyes, to take away our pleasure. I throw a rock at it. It caws off, back to the nests of when I was only seven years old and always afraid. But not now. Now, here, outside the butcher's. Here I am free and safe and fiercely protective. The bad omens are always one step ahead of me. I chase them. They fly, laughing, under the hedge, up the tree, over the tops of the houses, and off, out of my life. Good.

The doctor is not convinced. 'Dig! Dig deeper.'

But my time is up.

There will be a story, greased evenly from start to finish, made of words that have been selected like tomatoes — small, hard, sweet, and a little tight. It has never been my worry that I will not be able to tell a good story or walk a straight line.

# 39

When I was a child I dreamed I was lying on the grass looking up at the sky. There was a tiny ball falling towards me that got bigger and bigger as it fell, until it was not a tiny ball anymore, but giant and iron and spiked.

At the tip of my nose it stopped, which meant it was morning.

The dream marked the beginning of my understanding of the word lucky, which has been many things since, mostly Chinese. Perhaps it was even my first dream. There is no memory around it. Just the ball, the sky, and the grass that I am flat out on. The grass is well watered and carefully mown. The sky is cloudless. There is the view up at the ball which is mine, and then there is the final shot in profile of my nose about to be met by an iron spike and its unconscious, which is mine also. I am outside my body and then I am outside my dream. It is morning on a day in my childhood that I cannot recall.

There are other dreams in the house before mine — ones that come out at the breakfast table to try and make me jealous. I listen with a poised spoon. There is no reason why that sort of thing should go on in my brother's sleeping head, but not in mine. I decide that it is time for me to have a dream of my own and so I do and it is about a bird and a lion, which is my own feeble spin on Æsop's mouse and lion fable.

'I had a dream,' I say. 'It was about a bird and a lion.'

This shows them that I am also having things happen. 'What happened?' my brother asks. I repeat that it is about a bird and a lion and then I continue to eat my breakfast. The next morning, and for many mornings following, I announce that I have had the same dream. Sometimes the lie comes out of my mouth before I even sit down at the table.

So when the spiked iron ball comes hurtling out of the sky and I realize that dreams aren't neat publishable narratives, I start telling the story of *the bird and the lion* dream, which is now worthy of italics, to anybody who will listen. And that is a lie because lies are hermaphrodites and please themselves with each other. I do not want to dream that my pillow has transformed into Solomon, who forces me to oil the hinges of my jaw. He is so beautiful to you. Believe me. My pillow is his cheek made of cotton so that I have to shake it, to wake it, it's morning. Breakfast is one orange. I do not want to dream that I have the skinned carcass of a bear inside a backpack and that I am trying a find a butcher to cut it up and sell it to his customers. But that doesn't change anything, because dreams come clapping.

The director wants a straight narrative so she can iron it and fold it and place it in a drawer. But all I can give her are straws. A box of red and white striped straws from the counter of a diner in Alabama. Straws and the beginning of a story about a bird and a lion.

'One day there was a bird and a lion. The end.'

She says that I need to give her something to work with. The people at the box office have already started selling tickets. 'Things happen,' I say.

They happen to people and then they don't happen anymore. The dream I lied about having sits on the cover of a book. And so it happened that the bird came across a lion and the lion said he had something to tell the bird and he told her a dream he'd had in which he'd *almost* been crushed to death under the weight of a giant iron ball with spikes on it. The bird pecked at the grain that the lion had scattered for her, cocked her head to one side and said,

'I've had a dream too — a dream about a bird and a lion.'

'Ah,' said the lion, '*the bird and the lion* dream. A good omen I think. Also a sign that you are not easily intimidated.'

'Let me sit inside your mouth,' said the bird. 'It's still early and the blackbirds aren't yet speaking about the sun.'

Once inside the lion's mouth the bird said, 'Do something to me. Anything you want.'

And the lion did something that he'd always wanted to do, which afterwards caused the bird to blush blood.

---

'The key ingredient of a good dream,' says my brother, older, smarter, dreamier, 'is nonsense. Stop trying to dream in straight lines. Let go of the idea of plot. Relax.'

That night I dream that I am a lion with wings, which, my brother spitefully informs me the next morning, is called a *griffin*.

# 40

I am just a girl. Let me be just that. Just a girl can't scale the wall. Just a girl can't thrash the wicket. I come up to my mother's hip. I lick it. The cake mix bowl is my reward for being 'the helper.' The tradition says lick the bowl while listening to your brother's cricket ball smash through the window of the shed. I put the bloody expensive sanitary pads in the cart at the supermarket and then, as soon as I get home, I strap them to my legs. They cushion the thrashing blow of my moods that try to stop the game early; they cushion me from the truth that my little hanging pepper just isn't there.

They thrash me to death — the white man and his white son — and I like it. I like the lawn's crew cut, cushioning their system — a system that ticks, tickety-boo, to the 24-hour clock. I stroke the horse of my stepfather's rich girl fantasy, sniff her sweet neck and wet it with my bottle of fake tears. I sweep the hearth for my swooning Cinderella mother, while she keels over in her too-tight bodice to let another girl, me, have a go at seducing the prince. There are never enough princes to go around. It's survival of the fittest and my weapons are always sharp and readily available. I whisper into my horse's ear, 'I need a groom to pin me down in the stable and a poison comb to run through the haircuts of soldier-traitors.' She nudges me forward. But when it comes down to it I always fail to take action, running away squealing when he smashes the wicket with his upper-class rage.

The girl is just a poor girl. Let her be just that. With the address of a rich cousin tucked inside a stocking and her calloused fingers smoothing down her work dress, she knocks on the kitchen door at More House. Is let in, set up, shown the ropes, tarted up, fed, and popped into bed. The maids' dormitory is a larder stocked heavily with thigh and breast and pussy. Some of the meat sags over the hill and some of the meat is yet to be tasted. But because the girl is the protagonist of this novel her meat is somehow better, fleshier, smoother and more exotic than the rest of the larder's stock. And, naturally, her appeal is known to everyone but her and kept perfectly concealed under the dirt and grime of her poor-girl disguise. She is poverty Polly, struck with consumption, battling to hold onto her soul as it tries to flee her body, flapping through the fug of her disease. I will drape her over the outstretched arms of Emily Brontë (or is that Charlotte?), who will hurry across the fields to wake the village doctor, with her siblings trailing behind, sobbing. And a heroine will be born.

She pokes around in Cinder's cinders, pretending to be poor and hard done by just so she can get down a prince's pants. She spends hours in her dressing room, smearing lines of ash across her forehead and cheeks and then cold-creaming them off again because they look fake. Domestic war paint has to be just right if it's going to snag a husband.

The girl is practicing her when-will-it-all-end sigh when her mother enters the room and says, 'What are you doing sighing about like a nit? Have you done the potatoes?'

Today is the girl's mother's birthday. She is turning thirty-two. The girl likes birthdays and Joey got to have a scene with his mother and Mr. Nobody so the girl feels that she should have one too.

She likes the way people are kinder to each other, and the way they try to remember, as many times as they can during the course of the day, to congratulate the one celebrating.

'Happy birthday, Mum.'

'You've already said that, silly. Now, where's your father?'

---

The girl is in the kitchen when he arrives, watching the frothy potato water rise in the pan, just to the top, then lift the pan for a moment and watch the water rise again. It is mesmerizing. Her father kisses her on her cheek with his beer-dampened lips and 'Where's your mother?' and 'Put the kettle on' slip out of his mouth as usual.

'She's in the parlour eating bread and honey. It's her birthday you know.'

'I know, silly.'

The girl drags the pan off the stove and turns to her father who has just pulled a rabbit, by its ears, out from inside his coat. She wants to be that rabbit, tucked between her father's arm and his belly, not thinking, not breathing. He places the carcass on the table as someone might do in a line of narrative. Then, as if reading the girl's mind, he pulls a box of chocolates out from under his other arm. He is a magician, as all fathers must be. The girl grabs the box and scans the picture on the front cover. It gives nothing away, only the flowers of women. It is the biggest box of chocolates she has ever seen, but it is definitely not something her mother will want. Her mother will be angry because she has spent her birthday sighing through the chores, huffing and puffing the fallen tendrils of her hair. He is a foolish man, the girl thinks. She will most likely scream at him, from the tip of a cold, clattering poker, to stick it up his fancy woman.

Later that night the girl comes down to the dark sitting room to rummage around the edge of the hearth for strays. They are dirty, but delicious.

---

It is easier to be a girl in a tree called Tom than a boy in a dress called Nancy, but not easy enough.

Sexed flesh is cumbrous and manacled. Milton knew this well. It was only after he went blind that the chains fell away and he discovered that he was neither male nor female, but rather a sweet concoction of both, folded here, protruding there, concealing buttons and pockets in surprising places — like his body was a waistcoat. His discovery led to a frequent bolting of the door to his study, and, on one occasion, the extreme embarrassment of one of his daughters, who he accidentally bolted *in* rather than *out*.

'What's it about?' asks the director, who has come up behind me to ruin my lunch break reading session.

'Either sex, or both, so soft,' I say.

It's about what it feels like to want to be a boy when I am not a boy; a man when I am not a man. It's about how when I asked my friend what it meant to want a really big diesel truck and he said it meant I had penis envy. It's about having brothers who were born right. It's about getting a guy to sit between my legs so that I can pretend that what's his is mine. If I was born wrong I am made right when I am writing. There is no reason why I should be happy with what I've got. Only there comes a point when one has to realize that wishing has its limitations, despite the innovations of science. A sex change wouldn't cut it. It won't take away the fact that my brothers sat for longer on my mother's lap.

My original plan, in the days I thought plot was a simple corset, was to put Joey into the girl and the girl into Joey. Smoothly looped by silky lines of meaning and connection, they would come to the page with a great "A-ha!" and be so pleasing, so clever. But they acted like buffoons in their new bodies. It was permanent masturbation. I couldn't allow that. That embarrassing animal. And so I forced Joey to curl himself up into a ball and to pretend he was not yet born. The girl puked. Every morning. It took such a long time for me to convince them both that sex was merely a construct, something to play with when there was nothing else to do — mainly because I wasn't convinced myself. They knew that it was in their best interests to hide out at the far reaches of my imagination — a place I rarely go to — while I sorted through the dresses and trousers, the pink and the blue, the carrots and the figs.

I cannot switch my people. My people have got to be mine and to have come from my experience. No amount of makeup, name-changing, buttoning and zipping, snipping and dying, stretching and widening is going to turn them into strangers. They have the right fingers and when they look in the mirror they see that their fingers are good. They fly at their blue and pink booties drooling happy saliva. They click around in their spats and top hats and stockings. Sexed on the outside. Unlike rabbits which must be turned over and examined. Press a button and a tiny rabbit penis magically appears. Or not. *X* marks the spot of the mother. She goes into labour quietly and alone and then the father kills her offspring and it is my fault and I will go to hell for it.

Will my mother forgive me for all these years of wanting to get out of her sex and into the other? 'There are more than two,' she says, 'and you can be all of them.' My mother has thrown the towel into the fire, has pulled the mucus plug to let the baby out, has given the shove to nobody worth mentioning here. And suddenly the clouds are shrouding us while we change. And there we come. We come different. We open up all the beds. We gather in all the right places and nothing happens anymore at the place where the left leg meets with the right that splits to show that we all have an anus, which is what brings us together. Brothers and sisters. The finger pushes into the hole and tells us that we are all the same. On our stomachs. With our groans. In our orgasms we are all boys and all girls. In our curious hands fall away the signs of each other's sex.

There is no preference, only pleasure.

# 41

Hannah comes into the kitchen and asks the girl to take her fingers from her ears and face up to it, for a moment, like it is a *real* story. And it is. It's the way she swaggers that pisses off the other girls, so Hannah has decided it is time to tell her underling which bells to ring and which to muffle; when to strut and when to shuffle.

The girl has taken it upon herself to make the most of her servitude by being always outside the confines of the script and the plot. She does what she pleases. But her independence looks silly against a backdrop of Historical Fact. Everybody in the house knows what has happened — the larder, the rape, the son, turned lovemaking, turned loveliness — and none of them have much sympathy for her, not even Grace.

A whole shelf of jars are being ignored. The door of the larder is being ignored. There is a mouse cutely cleaning her face, but we are not interested in such kitsch. What matters here for the moment is the 'Oh!' of the girl's mouth which has just been slapped silent by the cook's plump hand. And that's malicious. And that's not in the script.

'Snap out of it!' says Hannah.

'It's all about being æsthetically pleasing,' the girl says, hand pressed to her now red cheek. 'And I'm not worried because he likes the way I look. When we marry, I will look fine in white.'

Now we marry. I am fine. White.

For pity. For love. Before, she couldn't get her skirts *up* fast enough and now she cannot get them *down* fast enough.

Blinded by an imaginary veil, she hugs her skirt tightly to her legs, hoping she can erase all the activity that's been going on *down there* in time to convince the wedding guests that her cherry is still plump, un-split.

She makes a last-minute decision, without consulting the director or myself, to keep everything down where it belongs. In place. I tell her that her good intentions will only get re-routed by my sense of humour and my obsession with porn, but she is adamant. She knows the Lord better than I do and says she has him wrapped around her little finger — a pretty red ribbon, reminding her finger not to bleed to death. 'Stay alive. Stay alive. You can do it!' shouts the rest of her hand.

Love is always a wound, picked at and kept open by fear. Nobody wears the pants. Or the trousers in Britain. Nobody has the upper hand or can wrap an entire human being around a single finger. But the girl is naïve — something I'm not happy with. 'So begin again with the line "But the girl is street-smart,"' says the director. Frustrated. 'It's not bloody complicated.'

Hannah isn't happy either. She has run out of advice. She used to be smooth. Fair. A hissing, but harmless goose. But somehow it doesn't matter now. She is sick of being typecast as the fat mother of people's bellies and wants to send the girl to supper with no bed — not realizing that this is exactly what the girl wants: a quiet night in with a book, a bottle of wine, and the sound of her own mouth chewing.

---

There is a woman with frizzy hair, who looks a bit like a horse, who's been standing just off set for the whole novel. I'd feel bad if I denied her a part.

'I stole this horsey cow from a Jane Austen TV series years ago. She's been hanging around. What shall I do with her?' I ask the director.

'Well, we need someone from the upper classes to contrast with the girl's ridiculous notion [the director raises her eyebrows at Hannah and nods and Hannah does the same back] that she might actually marry someone from another class. It just didn't happen in those days. And he raped her. Is that normal? To marry your rapist?'

'That was pages and pages ago. We're trying to shake off that narrative,' I say.

The director isn't listening to me. She's taken the horsey woman aside and is running her through the next scene. I sit down on the floor. To watch.

'And . . . ACTION!'

Jiggling in her carriage. Drunk on her own importance. She passes off her suitcases and offspring to Solomon, so she can fluff around in the arms of one of the Lord's longer, dirtier jokes; so she can get him to put his hand here, not there, here!, and then get the whole house to listen to her shrill prattery. The uses that women can be put to in drawing rooms are enough to make the maids — who are trained to pass through like drafts — want to vomit.

'And that's who you think you are,' says Hannah, 'which is impossible because you don't even have a name. Let alone a title.'

I'd like to say at this point that I think we ought to let Hannah read what has been written up until now, just to get the inside scoop on the shocking degree, albeit imposed quite arbitrarily by me, of the Lord's desire for the girl. The record is extensive. Even now he is spying on her from behind the kitchen door. We'll shoot him looking and then we'll play it back as evidence.

Hannah is annoyed. More House is crawling with maids who think that by getting in on the Lord's sexual circuit, he will suddenly drop his addiction to variety and marry them.

'Emphasis on the word *them*, my girl. He is not interested in you! He has his pick of any girl he wants, whenever he wants!'

'Oh, but he feels differently about me,' says the girl.

'That's what they all say, love.'

But, upon following the direction of the girl's glance, Hannah catches a glimpse of the Lord peeking into the kitchen, at which point she admits defeat, throws her arms up, almost in a reverse-akimbo fashion, and leaves the girl to get on with whatever she's planning on getting on with.

The girl is fast becoming the star of this show. (*I'm* even convinced by her charisma!) Her dressing room has been expanded to make room for the constant stream of presents that the Lord has been sending. Sweetmeat. Silk lines of reason. The feathers of wealthy peacocks. And poems. Poems that we cannot write here. Poems that blush.

# 42

There are lambs here because they were there, every Easter, when Granny let us into her house by opening the door at More. Childhood is open to investigators with visitation rights. And what I think I am doing here, because you seem to be asking, is surveying the land because I want to build on it.

Is she in control, like a visionary, of her narrative — 'Here's where the story ends' — or is it in control of her? Is she pregnant with a paperback? There's a danger in this kind of thinking says the cliché and it's riding on the back of a lamb and will snap it. Break it in its tracks and stop it before it makes a right turn out of this memory. But come, come. Granny has a lot of books, and it is a shame that I only open the ones with pictures of tits and larks. I rise off the settee and ask my sister if she wants another book.

'Are we rich?' she says

'Yes!' I say. 'Look at the size of this library!'

I map and worry over the rise of my mother from the coal mine to the doctor's surgery. She's a skimmer and we hold on to her en route. I move out of this library with my sister as a tail and grind into womanhood on the skinny, black strap of the lady's watch that Granny gave me, but not until I have something valuable stuffed up my jumper — something that makes Granny's assumption that all poor people are morally corrupt not an assumption after all.

My stepfather, Granny's son, gathers coins from pen pots and under couch cushions so that he can buy us some Sunday sweets. I weep for the drama. Being poor is romantic and can be lorded over people who aren't. I tell my friends the story about the near brush with sweetlessness and they want to know how it felt to have parents who couldn't afford to keep me in fillings and I say that it was hard, but that things are better now. And as proof I rustle the Laura Ashley bag I am carrying. I am only 11 but imaginary children are already gathering around me to pull on my skirt and say, please mum, let's go. I ignore their whines, but have the sense to tussle their hair between my fingers and this shuts them up for long enough for me to tell everyone that I have picked out some excellent aubergine cushions to go with the chesterfield. I love the way it hangs. Bring out the fluted crystal. Huddle up to the Aga with mugs of Darjeeling. Hang herbs up by their ankles. Train the roses to fuck the trellis. And then make me your pink and eligible daughter.

In the beginning of their relationship my stepfather took my mother to the health food store and bagged her up with millet and molasses, which to her meant love because her babies were waiting back at home with their mouths wide open and their teeth sweet.

Raised by a man who hated the Queen for reasons that were entirely out of her control — that she had too much money and was born outside of Yorkshire — my mother grew up to be a socialist. But when a little money fell into her magpie mouth it woke the fox inside her. A pretty fox that cocked her head to one side and said, 'Maggie Thatcher isn't that bad. She's done a lot of good for this country.' My stepfather fed her the story of the autobahn and she looked at the silver-lined fascist vein that pulsed in his temple and it fascinated her. She kissed it good night and good morning. And magically her wardrobe filled with shoes and ripened with linen and silk.

Us girls like a big, fat fascist. We like the thrust of his cigar, his fist of green bribery, the 'What'll it be, doll?' and 'Bring the lady a cocktail.' We slurp up our expensive drinks, our legs shortened significantly so that we can swing them freely under the table. We accept that Daddy has a job to do. A big job. A big, dirty job that ain't fit for our eyes. And that's absolutely fine! Just as long as we can go shopping. Shopping in the sweat shops. Shopping in the put-it-in-the-fucking-basket shops! Shopping in the shop-till-you-drop shops. Shopping in the diamonds-are-a-girl's-best-friend shops.

My mother, exhausted, placated, sucking the milkshake out of her marriage, tells me to take the bags to my room and hide them under my bed. She works hard. She wins bread. She is a boss and a serious business women. But this doesn't change the fact that her husband, coming up the stairs jingling change in his pockets, will put her over his knee and spank her if she doesn't hide the shopping bags. Quick!

As I slip the bags under my bed I learn one thing — that women, even when they are spending their own money, are being naughty: mother bird brings baby bird a worm. That's the end of the story. Unless we consider Part II, which is about how mother bird flies off to find baby bird a second worm.

Neither Joey nor the girl come from a rich family, although the girl gets to work in the home of somebody wealthy. I prefer them poor and that is my prejudice. I like to know that their concerns are my own. There is nothing but poverty to stop me from writing and so I have to make a choice. This book has been a long time brewing. Cold, it tastes like shit. I've thought about marrying for money, but then I'd be too busy shopping for chintzy silvery things to have time to write this. My privilege is this hour and it is my finest.

# 43

Here is a meeting in a drawing room between the Lord and a visiting Lady. A new one, prettier than horse-face, but just as annoying. Outside, a fence is being constructed, each blow of the hammer hits nerves in the chewy roots of the Lord's hangover. One English splinter and one Canadian sliver find their way into my mind. I need a needle to dig them both out.

The Lady's skirts rustle over the new butler's shoes. The swan is a fine bird. She attempts to emanate it, despite its large wingspan, opening her arms to embrace the Lord. The Lady, arms gorgeously silk-coated, scandalously licks the Lord's neck.

A sliver of knife-light vies for a place in this narrative. Hannah has sent for the knife sharpener. He cycles up to More House — a momentary flash in Miss Marple's peripheral vision — thinking thoughts that I am unable to pick up because he is not part of this book. But while I'm here I might as well give him a stern face, broad shoulders and a slightly crooked nose from fighting with his brother in a movie I saw called *Inventing the Abbots.*

The knife sharpener is sweat and pornography. I catch him with my big eyes, my mouth slightly open. I am taking second glances at secondary characters. Someone please remind me where the show is. I'm twisted up in the velvet curtains. Luxurious as they are, they have the odour of popcorn and hands that have come in from the garden and are yet to be washed.

Let's call it lust, for now. Later it will probably wear thin when I find out that the only thing he likes to talk about is knives: knives for the jungle; knives for fish gutting; knives for crimes of passion.

Now, swing everything back to the Lady. She is certainly up for a little drama, having attended the best acting school in New York.

The Lord is pleased to see his hands in the mirror behind the Lady, palpating (yes, that is the word I have chosen) her pompous ass. Also in the mirror he sees the girl standing by the door, wilting to follow out the next order. She has farted and is hoping the Lord and Lady don't come too close to her smell.

A bird is hopping in the garden, close to Emily Dickinson's leg. The knife sharpener is leaning his bike against a fig tree. I split a fig in his mind. It is before the fall. Fig leaves are not yet being held responsible by their branches. The moment is asking to be filled. And that's my job. So I'll ease off on the distractions for a moment and give you a scene:

The scene that is about to ensue is sexual so get your hand ready. Hover it over your belt buckle, button fly, zipper or waistband. I will not bring in anything disturbing or abnormal.

'And . . . ACTION!'

Wait! Wait, wait. I don't like the way the Lord has swanked his hair back this morning. It's like he's trying to look younger than he really is. The girl still hasn't been given the order to leave the room and that's bothering me, too — like a fridge that has been left open in a movie — especially because I know that right there in the script there is the line, 'That'll be all, Miss.' He's keeping her here for some reason, but keep the cameras rolling. I want to see what he has planned. It could be good. He did attend the same New York school that the Lady did. In fact, that's where they met. It was a cold autumn afternoon. They were spilling out of the stage door when deep in each other's television screens they saw a talent that was impossible to miss. At once one took the other by the hand through a hot chocolate, a rusty-treed park, and a long session of lovemaking. She was wearing knee-high brown boots over blue jeans and a huge brown sweater. Her slim legs poked and pranced out of the bottom of that fluffy number. She was virtually Diane Keaton. 'That'll be all, Miss,' he said, once he'd cum, which was a line from the play they had been rehearsing that day and so that made her laugh and god! did she look pretty when she laughed. He wanted all of New York to see that smile.

The Lord asks the girl to kiss him in front of the Lady and that makes the Lady mad. She fills her face with blood by hanging her head upside down and then screams at the Lord that she will knife him in the heart if he doesn't tell the fucking maid to leave the room. Her teeth are spittle. The whole red, angry mess of her face is quite disturbing and Makeup must certainly be given a thumbs-up for that.

'That'll be all, Miss,' the Lord (finally) says. And the girl leaves the room, glad that they haven't mentioned her fart.

The girl is halfway to the maids' quarters by the time the Lord catches up with her. He kneels on the step below hers and grasps her black-and-white French maid outfit with his pleas of please forgive me please.

'It's only a movie! Fiction!'

Cut to the bird that is about to touch Emily Dickinson's leg, but is startled away by the knife sharpener turning his bike on gravel. She turns. Emily, not the bird. He gives her a dirty look that she particularly relishes but that doesn't leave me with much to go on, as I'm not sure what I mean by *dirty*. *Good* dirty or *bad* dirty? Funny as in *ha ha* or funny as in *strange*?

Cut to a window shot, over the girl's left shoulder, temporarily entitled *The World Insists Upon Miles of Cold*. Nothing about the Lord's hands can warm or soften her. It is her curse upon him to love her. A curse that I am almost tempted to lift, because his childhood was hard; because I am a total pushover. I need to consider it over a mug of Darjeeling.

'Put the kettle on, darling.'

# 44

Joey has been dying to get out of his body and into the girl's, but he knows all too well that the cliché is too well known around these papery parts for anyone to bat an eyelid. He's addicted to recycled narratives. Rather than use his imagination, he is content to scavenge on the slagheap of English Literature. With me.

If you look closely, you can just about see him now, scraping at the earth with his nails for the baggie of your favourite drug that he hid yesterday — just after he saw the dead woman. We know that. But we also know that she saw him. Lifted the lashes of her acting eyelids so slightly that he didn't notice he was being watched.

It is the first day of spring—I go with the season that pleases. Creatures are giving birth and being born in the hedgerows. The soil is alive with motion that we are able to see in cross-section because I've brought along my worm farm and have stuffed the world into it. If only the worms knew how to conduct business. They'd be rich. One passes over Joey's stash — completely oblivious. The lane is humming. The trees are whispering. The onomatopoeia is disastrous. Every school kid in England is writing a poem about spring: 'Spring is springing / golden ducklings swimming / daffodils bursting / children laughing.' 'Well done! Four stars!' writes the English teacher. A duckling bursts the drum of a tulip that has been kicked down by a frolicking lamb. With its brand new beak. The day is widening with possibilities. We are far from the house where Mrs. Nobody is peeling and dicing potatoes for the stew must be ready by five. She chops them too small in her worry so that they crumble on her husband's complaining tongue. We are in the woods and lanes of mapped novels.

I don't know what happens when Joey gets high. I haven't done the particular drug he does. So he'll have to do it privately, and he'll have to get it from a place I've never been to and from a dealer I've never met. And he'll have to just show me who he is in the morning after he's been up all night grinding his teeth and grinning. He'll show me his wide eyes and I'll know. He'll show me his snappy self-hatred and I'll know. But still, I'll lay the prettiest red dress out for him on his bed, with the sharpest pair of heels he's ever seen, like I have a clue what goes on in his head, because really it's that I want him to cross-dress, like I think it's funny or something, or because it works with the girl's penis envy via some unimaginative parallel structure that Literature students will be able to catch and match. As if I know. I do not know. There is the urge to sit behind him and have a go at it like it is my own. There is the disgust at my own genitalia for being so goddamn open. There is my brother doing Wonder Woman impressions; flicking off the living room walls in his skinny body. Delightfully dangerous. I feed the data into the hard drive and press 'enter'. The results are astoundingly close to the original hypothesis: We want out. Let us out. Let us be nothing to do with our mother's tragedy.

He takes the baggie from the earth and opens it. Zoom in on his dirt-stuffed fingernails. A sparrow on the hedge is checking out the scene. Nature juxtaposed with Science. He takes the poison like the answer to a question written confidently in a notebook. And one more question: What is it like to turn seasick cartwheels? As the ceiling flies away I see for one moment what is must be like to be slowly walking down the hall faster than the walls of the club lined with jittery youth are moving. The bathroom stalls are opening out upon aprons of vision and a girl who Joey fucked in my first draft — now buried by new, more modern words — drinks water and turns a whiter shade of me.

I was there, too, but I have forgotten the delight at knowing that I can dance through this entire life with my grin-face and look good no matter what I'm wearing. Everybody in this club knows I am out of my head. My head is fucking gorgeous! Where the hell is it? It is no wonder that Joey floats past the scene of the crime. He is more concerned with his stash than with someone who is already dead. People die.

The director and I didn't prep him for Scene 1. We asked him to improvise. It is no wonder that he hates his job. The dark room his parents gave him at the back of the house where the sun never comes is always crying. Only when Joey is straight do I give him something to live for — the Yorkshire Moors with god's light shooting daggers through the clouds or an orgasm or a mirror. That he made. That he made his own vision out of toilet paper rolls and pipe cleaners is admirable and so I always say 'Yes' to anything he wants because I love him like he's not my son. But my brothers. And I dust my hands off of their absence and give them back their drugs.

When Joey runs to the window dressed as a Victorian Christmas child, I bring out the snow machines and give him the greatest flurrying answer to his question that I will not desert him; that I will be here, always making him up pretty and pushing him out at the wide, wide land with the answer to the question he keeps asking me about how he looks in green being, 'Yes, you are a tree. Yes, your roots are deep. Yes, I will keep Mr. Nobody distracted with a bit of clean-shaven leg while you run away.' Run away. Run!

The train station is a mile from here. For this paragraph Joey is living in Deal, where scum from the channel ferries decorates the beaches and tourists lick fatty ninety-nines. Joey is aware of a man walking towards him, just a moving shape in the distance for now, but soon to turn into a policeman or a murderer or a pervert or a father. I push my hands down into a tank of fish, run my fingers along their scales, searching for a fair bone in my body. Fair of face. Full of grace. I waver nervously, at the end of every chapter, towards forgiveness; ready my hammer to strike down the pigeon holes I've stuffed men into. Their backs have snapped. They feed me honey and drugs. I get off my face and fall into the lane with a loud suicide smack. My cheek is blood and gravel and the last thing I see before I kick over my bucket of prejudice is Joey, scrambling under the hedgerow to his freedom.

Most of what Joey does, he does when I am not there to watch. Nor are you. Nor are his parents. He spends much of his time alone. He stares at the ceiling like we all do when we are scaling the mountains inside our heads. There are stars on his ceiling. Dreams waiting to burst into life. I do not know Joey very well, so when he runs off the set of this book, the only choice I have is to let him return when he's ready. When he does, if he does, I will let him know that I've fitted his hole with a pigeon. Rightfully. A prize pigeon — one that is trusted to deliver love poems into the right hands.

'It's not that bad in there, is it?' I ask.

'Coo,' coos the pigeon, which means yes and or no.

# 45

As is the case for most child runaways, there is nowhere for Joey to go. He wants back into this book. Delighted that he has taken back the responsibility of personifying the gunk from my subconscious, I wrap two paper wings around him, which I rustle for the sound technician because I know how delirious a sound like Rustling Paper Feathers makes him.

Joey sits beside me in the belly of the girl. He is yet to be born. He is starting again. At one point or another I am going to have to whittle him down to a coherent shape. He is kicking and that's good because it means he wants out and I have told the girl that when he is born I will stop this writing lark. What I do not realize is that by the time she rises into the arch of her labour, with us watching her on our backs in the long hospital grass, I will have become an addict to my daily hour.

Joey demands that I catch all my clichés and stamp them out for good. He is sick of the words I use. I treat them like accidental props, found in a prop-box at an Amateur Actors Society meeting. He has told me he likes the story bits, but that he gets embarrassed when I put him into the weird bits or the bits that leave the cast and crew wanting to know what happens next.

'Nothing,' I reassure him. 'It's OK, Joey. Nothing happens. I am not going to let you get plotted to death; let you end up howling around your lover's window with heather in your hair. That wouldn't be fair. That's why your better ideas are being let like blood from the arm of an Elizabethan farmer into this bowl that is pulp and bleach. You nurse me with ideas. I take what I need and then burp. Your tit is mine. *Tu casa es mi casa.*

'We need to talk, Joey. We need a little space. I cannot tell what you look like in the mirror because when I look I see myself. And it gives me the willies.'

'Are we done?' he says.

'Yeah, we're ready to go home now,' says the girl.

'Not quite,' I say.

# 46

British Columbia is on fire. There is nowhere to put the girl without singeing her stumps. She is in my trailer and I'm sorry about that, but it has come to my attention that writing a novel is about control. I do what I want with her, when I want, because she is me and mine. I take her for myself because she knows that I'm behind the scenes, talking to the costume designer about rising her up from the coal.

'Darling,' she says, like a movie star — because she is a movie star. 'Be a pet and bring me a mineral water.'

I tell her to call me 'love' or 'put the kettle on, love.' I am common. I was born on the green, green commons down onto a patch of three-leaved clover and I loved her when I made her and I think I love her now.

'Love,' she says, like my mother, 'what are you thinking?'

I'm thinking that there's a slaughterhouse on the hill. A million chickens are getting their necks wrung and for what and for nothing. I'm thinking that cows have soft muzzles that kiss grass out of my hand; that lamb without an article is baby sheep without an article. We pass the slaughterhouse on the way to the set. The blood is nosed towards gutters and drains by men with hoses and brooms, wives and children.

'I am thinking about the slaughter of animals and of characters. What is it you think I am here to do?'

I know that the girl wants me to guide her, but I'm tired. She says nothing.

'You're dead,' I say. 'And live in the breath that drives a couple of words through the mouths of a couple of people. I am not driving you. This is no resurrection. I just want to fall in love with you. And keep you. Joey too. You are the two perfect halves of the whole that is my Prince Charming.'

But I am slapped by the sudden slap of a thought that they're both starting to wilt out of character. Her black dress, stolen from my mother's closet, is bothering me now. It comes from a former time; a time I thought I *had* to be my mother or no-one at all. I quickly put the girl into a blue dress, a particular blue, the colour of the cover of *Debbie: An Epic* which I just saw out of the corner of my little eye where it lives like a bee. There is no mourning now. Joey's suit comes tailored of the same material. Leaves for lapels, for crowns. Wrists flecked with a colour we cannot replicate because nature has taken the recipe and swallowed it, forever. It is perfect. Beyond the reason of the meadow. A word in a sea of babble. I dress them. There is nothing I like more than the material they are made of. I fold their patterns and hide them in my bra, smooth them down and ruffle them alive again. My need to play in full swing.

The girl stands behind me as I write this. She has her hands on the back of my chair. Joey kneels in front of my chair, his head blocking the screen, his fingers on my keys, trying to make his life readable, real. We are a chariot and the last to cross. The line is forming.

'There is nothing for either of you today,' I say, feeling a bit better at the idea that we at least have a shape and a tarot card: The Chariot. Aries. Direct, sure of our one singular self, wood, wheel, flesh, hair, tail and mane.

They have to get out of here before we start something that I cannot stop, that I have to commit to. They make the need in me to matter and they decorate it with marzipan, icing, jellied diamonds. We are a big cake, buried in the missionary position with my missionary boyfriend trying to pump God and meat into me. 'Christ,' I gasp and 'Oh God,' get me out of this bed and into 1814 with a candlestick holder and a white fickle nightdress coming off and coming on in every room of More House.

The Lord is striding towards me in boots. The story is now back on.

He stops in front of me. I am tall. Our noses touch. Our eyes cross. We take up our positions for the next dance. He has been trying to get back here all night.

'You've been ignoring me,' he says. 'Why?'

'Christ. Give me a break. You think I've got time for any more lovers?! As it is, I've had a go at the entire cast and crew,' I say.

'I was referring more specifically to being ignored as an actor,' says the Lord.

'Oh.'

'I was wondering if you could draw out my character a little more? He's fairly static. Always billowing and striding and lusting, but not much else. He never really says anything of any significance and all he does is come — in all senses of the word. 'Here he comes. Striding down the hallway. Whipping the tall grasses with his riding crop. Heading to the larder. Coming on the nightdress. Ejaculating on the maid. Shooting, merrily, into the mouth of the poor lass . . . '

He is reading from a script that I did away with ages ago because it wasn't technical enough.

'OK, OK, I get the picture. You want more lines. Fair enough. Go and have a word with the director. She's in trailer 4.'

On his way to see the director the Lord runs into the girl. I have her leaning against the wall of the house. Her eyes are closed and she is sunning herself like a lizard.

As he approaches, setting the gravel to barking, she opens her eyes. 'What manner of man are you? Throwing intoxicated stones at my trailer window last night?'

'A horny man perhaps?'

'I did let your fingers in, but not willingly. The thing is I am not a good lover when distracted by better lovers. You had my half-asleep-not-interested self, but you didn't have me.'

'I gathered as much. You being Mary, Mary, quite contrary.'

She ignores his comment. 'There was a single black hair on my pillow this morning. A kinky one. Is it yours?'

She has taken it from her pocket and holds it out to him.

'Yes, I'm afraid it does look like one of mine.'

'Take it back then. It's making me sick to the stomach.'

He takes it and puts it in his own pocket, and because the girl is now ignoring him, scribbling notes into her hot pink diary, he feels shy and stupid and decides to move on.

'See you later,' he says.

'Yeah. See you.'

After the Lord has gone and the sound of gravel has been switched off, Joey walks on set and stands in front of the camera. Close up. The girl a distant memory — Girl Against Wall — in the background.

'What have you got for me?'

These greedy good-for-nothing actors, who think money grows on trees and good ideas flow in bubbling streams, are my creations. I write their names on a piece of paper, fold it up tightly and then swallow it. I pretend they are dolls and soldiers under my bed who come alive only when I'm not there. Conveniently.

# 47

Joey is riding his bike home from school. There are things worth looking at. Clouds that make him think of white trees upside down, on the verge of uprooting themselves and drifting down to earth, a drooping blanket of fresh ivy, forbidden girls in their go-ahead skirts.

The gallery on the corner of the street is exhibiting the infamous painting *Girl with a Ham*. He knows his mother is working, filming a different scene — one that doesn't involve him or 2009 — but he loves to watch her work. This is their first movie together, but they've worked together countless times before in novels such as First Draft, Second Draft and Third Draft.

He passes the butcher's shop and sees the two butchers there. One is Helen's father. I know him. He's the one wearing the bloodiest apron; the one waving and laughing at me. I like him. When I return to England years later he has sold his butcher's shop and is working as an undertaker. Still close to blood, to skin he can touch without permission, but without the cleavers.

I wait on the curb in a vegetarian mood and smile back at him — only because I have manners. The girl passes out of the shop. Up the dark high street a painting is forming. It will later hang in an art gallery:

*Girl with a Ham.*

The vines come at her over the flint walls of a graveyard. She is thinking of digging a grave for the ham — to appease me and her Jewish relatives — but knows that Hannah will be angry if she returns from the village empty handed.

Today I especially love the blue of her dress. Blue is the only colour, that when mixed properly, can get me drunk. When the embroiderer takes up her blue thread I always watch to see what she is going to do with it. The song of her sewing might be a metallic, electric blue — the colour of dangerous gases — or perhaps a milk jug blue — the colour of Amsterdam.

Let's focus, Joey. Look around you. What a great earth! A bird scans it for you. I am sure that your hair is brown and your eyes are chocolate on my fingers at Easter. You have legs. I love them. Somebody wants to photograph you with winter rushing out all over, your hair is brown and your eyes too. Some pants look better on some boys. Hang right. Lean on your right elbow and follow the black line I am drawing up the high street runs the winter after her sluttish, giggling daughters. I have mown the lawn for you. Let it get at your bare feet. That equals summer. While fresh ivy equals spring.

Turn, turn here, Joey, and lay your bike on the front lawn. Wait a while and see what happens. I need you to look casual. Remember the riding-the-bike-with-no-hands look that did so well in the 1980s? That's what I want — minus the bike. See what I see. Then map it. Take the road down in pen and into the next village.

# 48

I let the girl alone. Give her some breathing space. Place her on a lonely hillside in period-stained period dress in the path of a simulated wind. I tear up all the harebells that are bothering me and give them to her with their roots dripping earth. More blue.

The girl's knotted hair is coordinated with her knotted scarf. She's been out fucking. It is winter. Her walk of shame is accented by her bed-head as is the fashion. The simulated wind blows right through her and comes out the other side sticky with alcohol. Freud, equipped with his forensic tools, holds a strand of her hair up to the light and nods. He places it carefully inside a plastic bag, which he labels *Hair Found on Pillow*. The light around this part of her body is just a fad. She is not the bright idea I thought she was, fit snappy by a lesbian tailor. Fit for London. She is a mess.

Solomon tells the girl she can pay for the drinks when she becomes a famous actress. Is it worth telling him, she wonders, that she already is a famous actress? No. She thinks it's better that she keeps up the illusion that she is a poor maid and a cheap tart. It gets her free drinks, enough to make her think it's OK to tell the actor who plays Solomon that I want to fuck him. Bitch. It was supposed to be a secret.

The girl's behaviour is reckless, stupid even. She flits between Solomon, the Lord and Grace as it suits her fancy — never loving any of them because she doesn't yet know how. The first rule of loving someone is to love yourself. This piece of Hallmark philosophy is more profound than we know. If we don't love something — ourselves, for example — we don't mind a little rape, a little punch, a little kick, a little putdown, a little infidelity. Just a little, mind. A pinch. Why would we? 'You need an old shirt to paint in? OK. Here's a shirt with a rip in it. You can wear this.' The girl is a shirt with a rip in it. She doesn't lay herself out on the bed carefully like tomorrow's school uniform. She stuffs herself into an art box until someone wants to make her dirty. The concept of self-esteem is completely alien to her. I have brought this to the attention of the embroider and she is going to see what she can do.

'I once was blind,' says the embroiderer.

'But now you see?' I say.

'Yes, but now I see,' she says. 'I was blind but now I see.'

'That's amazing,' I say. 'Me too!'

The girl is caught breaking hearts and asked to bring out her purse to pay damages. More House turns into a courtroom, so that every mote of dust can be seen performing its frantic dance — a contrast to the sleepy drone of her accusers. I bring in the set decorator and ask him to bring back Mrs. Schuster's generic margarine tub. All the maids on staff huddle around the tub crying and shuddering at the thought of the girl's dirty lesbian fingers.

I know too much. It is probably better for the director and I to work more on subtle innuendoes, rather than full-out expressions of lust. The director has been pulling me over to her camp, trying to convince me that by working together we might actually finish this film. She tells me that it's all about love. Does she mean love of the joy of the doing, love of the me, me, me, or love of the money?

I trip on a memory. I can't get out of the bags and their labels. Clear plastic. So easy to see through. I must make action. Do something that's been there and done that. Making something out of nothing but the word "Action!" is scratching at my nerves and making them wobble. I start. I trip. I like the feel of the grass under my body.

# 49

Fruit and sandwiches weigh down the basket that Granny is carrying. My brother and sisters and I hurry behind her. She herds us up into the barn loft, where she weights down a piece of flapping tarpaulin with some leftover bricks. Placing the basket in the centre of her makeshift picnic blanket she orders us all to sit.

'Eat your lunch here and keep the crumbs off the tarpaulin,' she says.

We are animals and she is cold. The fruity fruit is in us all and we are all Carmen Miranda lookalikes hoping to win the contest. My banana is slipping. My sister's peach ornament is chased by a swarm of bees up into the trees of a children's storybook. My brother is a hula girl. Granny is already back at the house pouring herself her elevenses — Stone's ginger wine with ice. Fucking hell what does she take us for? We are animals and she is cold writing paper before being written on.

I need somewhere else to go. I am sick of Deal. I am sick of the woods around these parts. I am sick of train stations. But mostly I am sick of Granny and her mansion — the only house in my memory appropriate for filming a movie starring someone as important as Lord Byron.

I rob More House of my cast and crew and take them west to the mouth of this river here, where we erect a pavilion and concoct cocktails. It's a hard night of drinking and too much is said. I understand the inconvenience of our move for both the cast and crew, but do nothing to water down their anarchy.

It's too pretty. Hot and pretty. And, besides, I am losing the thread on purpose.

Nobody knows where the girl and Joey are. Hannah says that she saw them going off into the woods around these parts. I figure that they've had enough of nothing happening. I want to follow them, but Hannah puts her hand on my shoulder and gives me that look that I created for her, so I pretend to head back into the tent to watch some Chinese contortionists.

---

'What's that in your hand?' says Joey.

And the girl says, 'It's a dildo that I made out of leather.'

'Why would you want one of those?' says Joey.

'I've wanted one since I was a little girl. It's not enough to be a girl. Being a boy is far better in this world. I want to have access to the right place and the deep thrust of the saying yes. But here I am with my penis on the inside, dripping red from time to time, waiting for a kiss from a snake. I want to be stationed in front of the right hole and released.'

She goes on and on.

'I've always wanted to be a girl,' Joey says. 'Because I've always wanted to have someone fill me up. I want to be stationed in front of the right cock, prosthetic or not, and have someone go at me until I'm up the pole in love.'

The sound technician pokes his boom into the noose of this conversation and gets their words tangled up with the sound of rushing water and owls. The woods reject them both. They reject themselves. But not each other.

'I'll give you what you've always wanted,' says the girl.

But when she tries, she cannot bring herself to do it because he is her son in one context, a murderer in another, and her co-star in yet another, so she turns to me, her arms akimbo, and says,

'Come on. Give me something to work with.'

It is almost time to stop and let somebody else have a turn. I have been pursuing this tail of distraction for years now. My grandfather may have been right. He accused me of being a pen-pusher and then he pushed me out of the pen and into the fold. He wanted to tidy me up, sandwich me between towels in the airing cupboard, smooth down the crease of my inherited rage. It made sense — to be as close as possible to the heart of the house, to be ironed out. But I was caught up in the spirit of my generation and prided myself on my independence. I went out, just to walk alone through his village, so I could be labelled as 'Seen' — a loose woman hunched over fluttering pages. Unfolded. Cold.

I tell the girl to write her own story, because she never seems to finish a scene is starting. Gather around it and 'Shush!' The world of sheep and lambs is huddled gluey to the scenery of a shepherd's red sky wishes. In the morning he will whittle a scene out of nothing but the birth of a lamb and he will call it an allegory. The girl is caught projecting stories into the future and told to curb her widening mind. She has stumbled upon the urge to sew; has clotted her thoughts and left them on the outside to be eaten by insects and vermin. The veranda is a bloody mess that keeps her busy until dinner. Broad beans darken and wrinkle in the boiling water. What boiling water?

# 50

Helen and I decide to go back to the kitchen. As a team. We wear aprons. Helen is chewing bubblegum loudly and has taken off her pink National Health specs in order to look more menacing.

Mrs. Schuster looks us both up and down with the same smug look on her puffy face that she wore in an earlier scene, in all my memories of her.

'Is this your lezzie friend?' she asks, sneering all over her crinkled-up hairy moles.

Helen switches on her zombie arms and legs and starts walking towards Mrs. Schuster. 'Kill–the–cook–er–y–teach–er. Kill–the–cook–er–y–teach–er,' she drones. She sounds and looks more like a robot than a zombie. We'll have to do a re-take later, but for now I like watching her rescue me. My zombie friend.

Mrs. Schuster isn't scared in the slightest of us little girls and turns to preheat the oven to gas mark 6, leaving us with the view of her lard-fattened ass. The Sarahs and the Carolines are huddling around her, fantasizing about filling their future husbands' mouths with cakey delights instead of pussy. They remind me of my inability to bake anything edible or to get through to final period without eating most of my ingredients. I start to falter.

Helen can see that I'm feeling intimidated and worthless, that the burning cakes of tomorrow will ruin the tiny speck of self-esteem I still have cruising around in my bloodstream. She puts her arm around me and says, 'Don't worry about them. They're all stupid cows. We at least know how to have fun. Look. What have you got left of your ingredients?'

I open up my biscuit tin of ingredients.

'I've already eaten all the jelly diamonds, and an entire block of marzipan, and I'm halfway through this block of baking chocolate.'

'Give me a chunk of that chocolate,' she says. I break her off a giant piece and she stuffs the whole thing in her mouth and starts salivating grossly, trying to get a handle on it. I do the same with an even bigger chunk. Quickly my teeth turn into stringy, brown laughter — a mirror to Helen's own face. We laugh loud, insane laughs, forcing the good girls to huddle in even closer to Mrs. Schuster. Then Helen hangs her lolloping marzipan block between her legs and pretends to mount me. We sizzle in the water. Our hatred fierce and funny.

# 51

I play Simple Simon with all the books I have ever read. Joy comes when I make a mistake and Simon stops, looks at me and, arms akimbo, crosses — just for my benefit — a smile with a frown.

Without imitation I wouldn't have known where to begin. My life can be tucked neatly into a paperback, then into the pocket of a boy (Jocy?) cycling through a sleepy British Columbian town. When he stops at the lake to read he reads an unwritten book. The only page that is finished is the first one. It says something about a woman who has been murdered. A cliché. Hurray!

When I wrote the first page I thought I could have gotten away with it. There were no better ideas. The first time I saw her she was smoking outside her trailer. A few days later I saw her shove her way through the extras to get on set, acting like she was the star of the show — which at that point she was, being a murdered woman and the first thing that came to mind.

'Who's that?' I asked the director.

'Who? The one in the she-deserved-it skirt and the she-deserved-it stilettos?'

'Yeah, her.'

'That's your alter ego, isn't it?' she said, looking down at her cast list.

'Oh yeah, you're right,' I said. 'Make sure she's killed off in the first scene.'

---

The identity of the dead woman has been discovered. She is my primary sex characteristics. The throbbing cunt, healed by the corner of a paperback thriller. She is a variety of pronouns. A toe tag. The adjective is *dead*. The verb is prostrate. Joey's accessories cling to her body like abandoned babes. She would never hurt a fly.

In her corpse is lodged a plot. It's still there. I haven't bothered to let it drag me through those Illinois woods to the hunter's house. I haven't let myself pick up the glove. She is a prostitute and her pimp will suffer a loss which he will wipe away with one swipe from his hankie. But he holds the glass slipper and she's its only filler. So let's bring her back to life. Prop her against Steven, prop him against her, and build a three-tiered wedding cake beneath them. We make and we kill. There is a time for. She is zapped back to life and straight into action, talking to a friend on the corner, tugging self-consciously at her skirt — unable to decide whether being lusted after is a good or a bad thing. Wiggling to her walkman in headlights, looking for love. There are no dead women in this book. Live with it.

# 52

It is hard work hauling Persian rugs and silk cushions into the theatre for the Lord to lounge on. Plus I'm out of grapes and other reasons to continue feeding this reel of language. God! Bring in the wilting roses from the hotel room of the recently-made-famous Tennessee Williams! Such a flurry of power. Such a powdery memory. So much applause after Blanche is blanketed by the silence of the asylum, that we cannot hear the ticking, ticking of our lives.

The stage is a gaping hole and spitting out of its dark centre come the girl and Joey. Churned up and out of sorts. The mirror spins in its frame — a frustrated widow fed up with looking at only herself — until she sees her two favourite people in the world and stops short at them.

Joey, the great actor, steps out on his soft, shod feet and delivers. The girl, mother of all heroines, wheels overhead like a flock of gulls. Her hair, tampered in beaks, is gothic and lovely. Joey orders his mother to come down from the heavens, so she can stick against the line of the script and him. She sighs, signalling my dad to lower her onto the stage, where the floorboards creak down the bird imagery into something much heavier, much more earthy and real.

Joey hands me a record and then he and the girl position themselves to dance. The sound technician rolls his eyes when the song begins. I do not recognize it. It is a song from a dream I am yet to have that has been composed by beetles and mice. It scurries over my heart illogically, opening the bottle labelled 'Cry'. I do.

I watch them dance, closer than they should be, but what's it got to do with me? I have stopped listening to my own promises and rules. I watch them dance, but half-heartedly, because I am aware that my empty wallet has turned into a mouse and is nibbling on my mind. To distract the mouse from taking me for all I'm worth, I stroke its belly kindly and say, 'There, there.' But it wants more. More money, more money. I worry.

Worry is a barking dog inside a head. Miniature, but anatomically perfect. It has puppies all the time and they bark too. Then they have puppies and their puppies have puppies. You get the picture. And so you drown them — ask the set decorator where he put the bag of kittens because you might as well drown them all together — and afterwards you clap your hands together gleefully because you know that there won't be any more worries. And then you get on with your life and everything is swell and hunky-dory until, one day, there is a 'Woof!' inside your head.

Eventually we all turn out OK — virtually worry-free. But for most of us OK is not enough. The platter of the future is permanently set in the centre of the table. It looks pretty. It looks sumptuous. It tells us to eat our gruel today and look forward to the impossible to pronounce dishes of tomorrow. We read the menu, select a meal and then wait. When it arrives it is never as good as the menu said it would be. A salad *lovingly caressed with vinaigrette*? An apple pie so authentic that *Granny will shit herself if she tries it*? In truth, the future is a lump of bread *gently accompanied by a glass of water*. Accept it and then be thankful when the waiter shows up with a salad made of edible flowers *daintily plucked from the garden of Eden*.

We are all worthy of betterness.

There, there. I will not hurt you. As long as we are all sick and dying together we may as well share the joke that is on us; may as well admit that all our animal intentions are scantily clad. We are hard pressed for opportunities to transcend our solitude and so we dance with anyone who will have us. We know that loneliness is the norm — garnished sporadically by a warm sleeping body, but we fight it with our blabbery mouths. 'I'll buy one year of getting in and getting out and after the year is up I'll buy another.' We are so glad that singleness is not a disease anymore — like it was when our grandmothers were young — but more a mild ailment, and in our joy we forget that our wombs expire. Before we do. I don't have to exchange one of my children for a box of chocolates, because I don't have any children; I don't have to stay with him just because he keeps me in hole-free stockings, because I don't wear stockings. All I do is get in and get out and get in and get out and stay lonely.

To comfort myself I dream up the fading click of my grandmother's shoes as she enters the Royal Opera House. She says 'Hello' to my father, who is still working there in this chapter, and heads to her dressing room. Sure, she often has to wave off loneliness with a bouquet of flowers, but as compensation she gets to feed at the platter like a queen.

I am in the process of discovering a way to empty the mirror of its sex and replace it with something more relevant — a look of forgiveness? As each draft blows away in the breath of the next, I pride myself in knowing that I am making pages instead of cake-babies; that I am beginning to love my fig more than I love his carrot.

# 53

The Lord is pink in the cheeks from walking up to meet the girl at the top of her hill. Things are making too much sense. There are harebells in the belle's hair and for a moment I am happy with the word 'pretty.'

The Lord is carrying a picnic basket that Granny has prepared, because he has never done anything for himself. He cannot love yet. First he must learn to love himself, to forgive himself the fingers of the creepy relative who bathed him when he was a boy — her pussy throbbing; who made him into a self-loathing predator. Darkness is manufactured out of darkness, light out of light, we are led by a blind imbecile to believe, so that we will accept it when we echo the failures of our guardians. They stand at the gates of the womb waiting to press our soft skulls into shapes that they like. Nobody tells us that the people around the hospital bed or out in the waiting room, are losers. Nobody tells us this. We have to figure it out for ourselves, but only after years of thinking it is our fault; that the fingers are part and parcel of childhood; that the sleazy uncles have just had one too many drinks and are not worth mentioning here.

I pity and understand the Lord, but I do not like him. He is not a child anymore. Kindness is there for the taking. If he wants it, he can have it. But, as usual, no-one is expecting too much from him, especially the embroiderer who pricks out his tendencies with a faint thread.

The plot is unfolding and flicking across the hills a good heterosexual scene that promises to get me off.

It takes effort to get Bessie up the steep hill to make these necessary furrows. Good old Bessie. We will root for her.

The gorse is around any time and any time I'll rip through it and tear the tights of my lines so that they run in many different directions and never stop running, wood pigeon. From these prickly bushes there's a rising that is happening. It's a growling love. My favourite. I cannot lie. She is getting weaker and there is something about his black curls that does her in. That gets her right here.

Solomon, who fell under the spell of a grape between my lips, and then lay himself out for me like a towel on a guest bed, is on the Downs this afternoon too. And so why not introduce him to the girl and the Lord who are gaily picnicking, discussing her most recent abortion (she's a modern woman now), and sharing an apple with an awareness of one another's spittle.

'This is my lover,' I say. 'He is very fond of his body. And who can blame him? It is smooth and rude. He likes the full weight of a body on his back and doesn't know whether that is a "problem".'

'You're probably not gay,' the Lord says. 'It's just that you like it up the ass. And who doesn't? And who wants it?'

The girl, as much a predator as the Lord by now, is up and reaching eagerly into the picnic basket for a carrot. Solomon is nervous but cannot say no to such a blue girl with blue flowers, asking. The Lord is bored and wanders off to sketch a wood pigeon that isn't there anymore for fear of men and their high boots and their long guns.

This is a wide blanket and a clear sky. Field workers are coming over the hill of a past century into an oil painting. Even Tess, gloveless, frosting the harebells with her turnip leaves has shown up.

Business is as usual and the girl has to be dreaming. She has never seen such skin! When I'm eighty I will think of Solomon's plum skin and that will make me a pervert. Then so be it. I was once traced by the breathless fingers of perverts.

---

They are curled up together on the blanket when the Lord returns. The jar of honey. One more bun? No-one wants it? Then I'll throw it for the birds. And the grapes are all finished except for a few that didn't grow properly and still cling — blackcurrants — to the vine. There's half a jug of cider left. Wishing he were drunk he gulps back another swig for Solomon is stirring. Through the haze runs a hare into her dear bells. And the woods are dreaming, swaying to Elvis' crooning. And the furrows are running down the field gaga over the promise of green. I cannot help noticing that the girl is smiling. The Lord wants to kiss her, but she is distracted by Solomon, and already warmly held in the arms of his afternoon. Everything about the sky is as memorable as an orgasm; it will keep us coming back for more. I pass the buck from image to image. Shift the visuals back and forth until they slip back to the earth as sand.

Coming up the field is the lusting Tess and we cannot blame her. Sparrows fall away embarrassed. Furrows widen. A beetle is learning to slow down and smell the dung on her booties.

# 54

The director has given me her director's chair.

'This might help,' she says, roughly forcing me to sit. 'Try and take control of your scenes a little more. I see potential. Lots of it. But nothing ever reaches a conclusion.'

I'm slightly depressed today so I say nothing. Just sit there looking at the room in front of me with its quiet Peter Pan beds, its on-stage charisma.

'What have you got written down there?' she asks, pointing to the wad of paper in my lap.

'It's my novel,' I say.

'Great. Let's take a look.'

She takes it from me easily because my hands are starting to melt with the depression and then she starts reading out loud. Quickly. Like she is checking off a list of things to do:

1. The maids have decided to drink red wine because it's premenstrual syndrome week at More.
2. The stairs to their bedroom are rickety under their sexy legs as they head up for a card game.
3. The Lord is away for the weekend — in London, showing off.
4. Hannah has gone home for the weekend, too. We can't have her fat floury fingers peeling back the sheets to check the girl's hands for evidence of masturbation. (She'd never really do that, but I've thrown her out of character for a second just to say that such things do happen. The horror!)

5. There is no knife-sharpener, either — rustling the gravel with his bicycle wheels.
6. And the new butler is barely a sketch gestating inside my pencil.

'OK. What do we need to get this scene in motion?' asks the director to herself. 'Last time I checked all the girls were freshly bathed and ready for anything. Let's do this.'

When the girls, who are getting paid the wages of extras, come in they seem to have formed a mini-gang. All of them chew gum and all of them looked bored.

The director preps them for the scene but none of them seem interested in playing any of the roles I've created for them. Marie, the newest and prettiest (in my opinion) recruit, thinks that I should start again from scratch and turn this into a murder mystery novel. She volunteers to play the murderer and immediately and stupidly gives away the ending of the book.

'I'll get him in that bloody tub of his!' she says.

Holly and Grace are arguing over who has the old maid, until they realize that she's still in the box. Also in the room are a few nameless girls. I will make sure one of them gets shafted with the old maid. Like the girl for instance. She's asking for it, not joining in, mooning out the window in an orphan mood for Solomon's plum skin. She's trying to steal him from me permanently, but I saw him first so she won't succeed. I turn her head back towards the centre of the room where the card game is going on and soon she is distracted by a story Grace is telling.

Suddenly the word 'suddenly' comes into the novel, which like 'meanwhile' or 'however' isn't really a word, but more of a broom clearing the way for a word. It sweeps in a knock at the door. A lovely, loud, unexpected knock at the door, with the sound of boys laughing behind it.

Marie gets up and opens the door to Solomon and some of his friends from the village. The girls are laughing behind her saying what do those bastards want and tell them we're having a girls' night. But the girl wants them to come in and so I have to please her. And, besides, I have never seen *him* — the one to the left of Solomon who is looking right at me and this is not my story so why do I keep intruding?

He has the face of a pixie, which means he has lived more than one life, and he straddles the border between male and female, leaning first one way and then the other, like an aspen leaf. Love laps at my heart its scratchy kitten tongue, waking up all my one-liners.

'This is my friend, the boy,' says Solomon.

The rest have names too but I'm not listening, because the boy is the same boy who combed apart the corn sheaves of my very first sexual fantasy. He returns to me now, lusting for wings. Me! Me! I will be the one to carry you upwards.

My eager, stupid heart races to the door to possess him. I put him in my car. I tap his darling past. I forget I am betrothed to a lovely man from the village, because my deep root is throbbing and my sweet heart is bursting and my sly belly sniffs at his sperm for babies. The boy doesn't know what has hit him. He is only an extra and this is his first day on set.

'Will I get paid for this?' he asks, now flat on the floor, passively letting me pull his pants down.

'Shut up and stick to the script,' I gasp, pushing down around him in a wet line.

The girls don't know what they are supposed to do and look confused, until the director rushes in (she is always rushing) and points the camera away from the boy and me. Our scene continues on its hands and knees into a future that I don't dare imagine, for fear of seeing how weak beauty can make me.

---

Solomon catches the girl's eye and puts it in his mouth. He is turning into her favourite carrot. He smiles and she smiles back. She smiles and he smiles back. Smiling is awesome. Sometimes it takes a cheesy line like that to really make her want to love a little, have another go at letting him in. He's knocking again. He's jealous of me, but he has no reason to be. I'm busy. I get off on the boy and then I get off the boy. He doesn't know what has hit him, but he needs the money and I'll let him hold the baby — once — when it's born.

I leave the room — a little pissed off. I thought of all my characters, and even gave some of them names, but they're more interested in playing cards than in watching me have sex. No one is interested in my daily grind. No one is pleased with the zigzag design I picked out at the plot shop.

The mirror is the only well-loved surface.

They play old maid for a while and share the wine they have filched from the Lord's cellar. They talk about things that are happening in the village that I know nothing about and play until Solomon is left with the old maid.

'She isn't half bad,' he says, licking her with his perfectly written tongue.

# 55

There is a strip of damp cloth that has settled just under my skin and is gathering spider dirt. I didn't realize that this was a sickness until I got home and attempted to think in lines and with purpose. But here it is. Heavy, swelling. Two arms pulling me down to the sickbed. The first reaction to illness is denial. I am writing to ask you to go away. My shoulders are breathing pebbles down into my tailbone. I must sleep.

---

I dream about drowning. There is only one drowning sea that all characters go to in the end. It's called *One Way or Another* and white sand has never touched my bare feet. So what? The pebbles that introduce the land to the English Channel are lush. Shush. And I do. Shush. And I listen, like you do, and ask you to hold my hand, because it's better that way. Shush. The beach is somewhere in Portugal and somewhere inside Sylvia Plath. There is the buoy and the fog and the lifeboat doctor. War. France on a clear day. The Goodwin Sands where they play cricket. Really! They play cricket! It is a lonely beach, late afternoon, heat trapped in the pebbles under my towel. Too much loathing at the pubic line; at my white parents and my subsequent white self. There is a hot dog buried in the sand. Strands of Gulliver's hair caught and fluttering over sea cabbage.

I am wrong to think that it is within my power to drown all my characters, like a sack of kittens. They are beyond me now — out of my jurisdiction — and they don't miss or need me. I must continue along the lines of yesterday, when everything either went according to plan or not according to plan, but was never a stream of consciousness meltdown. From the fever. I am still coming up from the fever.

The need for an anchor and a sailor's knot is clear. Even with the fact I have been wanting to dance the Lord down to the water's edge and into the sea, I am not convinced that death is ever a clever idea. I put my hair up pretty, bake one potato and eat it, just to normalize the situation. Then I bring his riffling hands out of my rah-rah skirt and organize his fingers. There is nothing I want more. Shush. This is a clear day. France is a sliver that speaks a different language.

The darkest part of my heart is a plum. Split, busy with a wasp. I run my finger along the cantaloupe seeds, part a slice of bread from her sisters and eat it. Normally.

# 56

I decide to drown only one character. In the woods around these parts. Outside of law and jurisdiction and border crossings. He is the runt of the litter and a British schoolboy.

Stunted, even before he hit puberty, by an introduction to adult lust, my stepfather never had much of a chance. Suffocating in the pillows of Freud's couch, he retold dreams of a mother who later became his wife and brought him children on trays to appease his appetite for their safe little bodies. In our arms, in our kisses, he turned seven years old again. Warm. Propped up against Granny with a story puffing its sweet breath just above his head.

At seven he is still a few months away from the event that would alter his and my family's lives forever and beyond. He is a little boy. Handsome. Serious. Intense. With a propensity to mischief and loud laughter.

I go to his house, disguised as my adult self. He doesn't recognize the stepdaughter he will later guard. He will know his fate and he will choose it. He did choose it. He has chosen it. I give him one chance to take my hand and step out of the line of his rotten destiny, but he pushes my hand aside and goes on with the story that has now come to be mine — even though I do not want it.

My stepfather is famous for his sneer and for his fluttering scarf. I recognize the way he pulls his socks over shin pads, over my legs, as he leads a boy from the visiting team to the pavilion of sugar. White plates. Roman Polanski gravel, of course — the most used sound effect for anything shot in Britain. Sugar for both the winners and the losers. Nobody cares who wins the match as long as it is followed by pink icing, cream-covered fingers and orange squash.

During term time he is surrounded by other sexualized children, made brutal in their mini-societies, where buttered toast is money and the housemaster is hardly economical with his semen. He exists in a little sea of howls and caps who should not be heard, surfacing only during the holidays to beg Mother and Papa not to send him back there.

---

When my stepfather drives us up to the gate of his old school, I can see an entire book in his eyes. He reaches his arm out of the car window and scans the scene, tidies it a little, and then pulls it into the car and onto his lap. From where I am it looks small. A model school. The chapel is letting out its boys all over his thighs. His crotch is a copse of sighing beech trees. It starts to rain. All the boys run across the courtyard and into the dining hall. Scarves flapping behind them in the wind.

---

The log over my unconscious is heavy, so he helps me to lift it and together we send it crashing down into the ravine of a song. Underneath we find what we are looking for — woodlice, centipedes, worms, ants, slugs, maggots. The sun blows her mood all over the shop. The insects are forced to seek refuge under nearby logs and leaves or to return into the earth. We sit together — his seven-year-old self and I — for a long time and we just watch and breathe.

'I am sorry that you ran faster than any other boy in your school, not because you were naturally fast, but because you didn't want to be raped anymore,' I say.

'Thank you,' he says. I want him to say sorry too, for everything he has done to me, my siblings, my mother. Without an apology it also makes my next line ('You are forgiven') look a little out of place. But he says nothing. He just sits there looking at where the creatures had been. I decide it is best to just go on with the story as it has been written.

'You are forgiven,' I say. 'Now, please, lie down here on this patch of earth and I will cover you with leaves and moss. Go to sleep and you will wake up in the next life with kind parents and a lucky clover birthmark on your left thigh. Treasure your second chance and don't take away the dreams of any children like you did to me and like I am doing to you right now.'

He willingly lays down on the earth and closes his eyes. I cover him slowly, ritualistically, with leaves that I have gathered especially for the occasion. I put blocks of sodden moss over his eyes, his mouth, his hands and his crotch. He lies very still.

'Go to sleep,' I say, softly. 'Stepfather never to be.' And he does.

# 57

The lines of family are not straight. Spill foreign blood at the kinks and then clean it up, love, clean it up. My line is a bloodied switch of birch against a thigh. My line is policed by an ignorant man in a La-Z-Boy, a map of whiteness that he cannot read spread across his lap and one, barely visible line of bitter froth along his upper lip. Newcastle Brown. To his right always sits a wife, a storyteller.

'Tell me the one about being related to the Black Prince!' I beg.

'Again? I am related to the Black Prince,' she says. 'End of story.' Her bracelets jangle in time with the jangling of her stallion's bridle. She is eighteen and sexy. There is a thick fog that lies over her land, but she spurs her horse through it at a gallop. Whenever she brings flowers to the tomb of the Black Prince, she rides her horse across the stone floor inside Canterbury Cathedral, ordering the Spanish tourists to get out of her way.

My grandfather also has things to boast about — like being related to every successful comedian, golfer and jockey from the north of England. At one point he has me thinking that George Formby is his dad.

The girl comes from those obscure times that we can easily poke our lines of legitimacy at and react with pleasure and phrases like — that's where I must have got my laugh from. My freckles. My stereotypically Jewish characteristics that always come up in movies. My stirrups and chain-mail. My club foot. My Nordic stamina. My one breast — the other having been lopped off to make shooting arrows easier. My dirty mouth. My *Lord of the Rings* costume.

The supermarket of ancestry — the place to buy all the right traits — is open for any loser to pretend that watching TV all night, every night has something to do with migrating across harsh tundra eating rotting caribou meat and getting frostbite. I am not sorry that I come from a dirty pool, because in my imagination I get to wear a sheepskin cloak and carry a pouch of rune stones while my pet falcon circles overhead. I scale the source of clean and fast running water. I put my hands in the water and I splash my face pretty and I kiss the hermit and make him smile and I dance on the Scottish rocks in my wet socks and the world spins and the babies are born perfect and I'm happy to be me and I'm happy that you are you — beautiful cold mountain you, my brother!

There is no reason to write my name under my mother's or my father's. Let's just stop all that nonsense right now. Somebody has to cut the line with a clean, sharp knife. Helen's dad would have a good knife if he were still working at the butcher's. He could undertake the deed and cut me adrift.

I see the girl waiting for me to finish telling the story about her long lark rise from poverty, up through the arms of a lovesick, violent Lord, into the crib of luxury, and then back, dipping back down into some cheap wedding ceremony with Solomon — a genuine local lad. I see her wanting me to leave her in peace where she can remain part of the trivial chit-chat of people in my family, who think that her having sex with somebody famous says something about our claim to the throne. This book is my throne. Look at me! Look at me! I am the worst of the bunch.

There are only stories to tell us who we are capable of being now, not then. Stories that we can lay, instead of names, at the feet of our parents, who worry that we won't be something worth recording. And there is love, there has to be, in the bursting hearts of my mum and dad, trying to do its bit. But when faced with such a filthy-mouthed mess of a daughter, dragged from the mill-weed of the ancestral pool, with her gills still fully operational and the urge to put a leather cock between the thighs of her main character that can point in any direction you want it to, things get complicated.

Shield me from the sunshiny sun of the sharpest memories and pretend, pretend that blood cannot pass from you to me, Father. That everything stops at the crowning, Mother. You were on the body then, not now, or later, just then in my first pop of life.

I get the chance to run away. Plus a head start. I run fast. I am ready for an end.

From the family that I refuse comes a house and a bookshelf. I can go into the house and take from it whichever book I want and I don't even have to put the book back. In the books I find others who are trapped inside their houses, and, like me, were given pens and paper as tools of escape. Outside the house is an imagination. I can go to it and I can thrive in its warm, lazy orchard. Bees will find me and sleepily bump against my body, but they will never sting me.

I grew up in the house that I refuse. I was given as much love as my parents could spare, just enough to allow me to jot down the word 'universe.' It wasn't until later that I transformed into my mother and went to live in a poem, and then inside the girl because she was my own creation and because it was about time; until I went into the night randomly, disconnected in beds from my own body, but never from his. I liked it sometimes and sometimes I didn't like it very much at all.

# 58

I am overcast. Even the strong bend and quiver. My mother gets under my skin. For the mirror she presents me with a baby carrot between my legs. Organic. I do not want to be this orange parody of a boy or have her hold me up, made up.

She tells me that men are more beautiful than women because they don't have to wear makeup. And with that out comes her little red or pink penis and her mirror. That is tucked. That is kept for moments like these when wives must decorate themselves against the fear of being less sexy than mistresses.

She holds me up so I can find myself in her arms, in her mirror. My fat baby self discovering for the first time what others see when they see me on my plush Buddha cushion, wearing nothing but skin. The landscape that is my face is immature. It becomes a race to see who can reach the glass first to kiss it, to lick it and say, 'Hel-lo, beautiful!' I am held up to the mirror above the fireplace in her hope that I will see me seeing me and thank her for it. Her strong arms charm me into a daughter. I do as she does. I carry her to every mirror and let her loose at my vanity.

And when I learn of the exactitude of my sex — X marks the spot — I am afraid to tell the costume designer that it's pink, not blue, because she has already sent my story to the embroiderer. Instead, I tell her to put Joey and the girl in the front alcove window to distract me, something for me to look at, to browse over for errors — cardboard cut-outs of my biggest fears: his and hers; male and female. Heavy with having to smile at their fates. I pull the edges of their faces back and down and force them to kiss each other with their beaked cardboard mouths.

I have spent these pages auctioning off the wares of my subconscious, until my mother tells me, using her warm voice — the one I will weep over when she dies — to stop hiding. She pushes me forward in my fat cuddle suit, making me feel ridiculously shy. But the set decorator is astute (today I like him even more than the sound technician) and clears a shushed path from my mother to the mirror.

My mother's charming arms free me into the mirror from my small world in which I am all lower body. In limbo. Wanting, but never having. I lick my own tongue. I press my cheek to my own cheek in deep sorrow over the lack of a penis. Around here everyone is licking their lack, their wound. We are thinking dogs curled into ourselves for fear of being booted out into the cold garden.

---

I steal a kitten from the suckling litter under the stairs, put her in front of my bedroom mirror and say, 'There you are.' (Pointing at the mirror.) 'That's you, see. See that there? It's you.'

See to it that you are there in the mirror and rarely anywhere else. Eyebrows. A dark green deposit between incisors. From the roof of the mirror falls a whole sequence of reasons to exist. For me. That visual. That queen of expressions. That finger really in there. That grasp for a small area of the stage, for the flattering fall of roses, for the bedroom song and dance routine and the keep it down up there!

At the end of the scene I eat the carrot. It tastes of me. My mother claps.

'Welcome home, love,' she says.

# 59

In the novel is felled a tree that hits a passing mouse and slides it out of its very skin — some soggy, panting bolus to be swallowed by a bear, with berries. The trees are dark, in oil, and carry the threat of owls. Brushing up against the sexy bushes flicks out a shower of needles that I put away safely into the cushion of Granny's wrinkled hand.

She doesn't flinch or notice, being a cadaver.

We say goodbye.

---

The Lord is striding down the hallway at More House with morning hair and thoughts of the weather. He's charming and I'd say beautiful when I put him between two maids and make them all pose, between better jokes, for the cover of my novel. And . . . CUT! Cut out the throat of the bird that sings in the poem. Cut out the face of the Lord from where his feet pass and then vacuum up the crumbs from his cheese sandwiches. He has not been here. He has not passed a hat stand here, a cat there. His image has been cut, but not pasted.

We say goodbye.

There is a blessed light that comes this morning to tap on the hall windows to be let in. Have your say, sweet light, and then tell me where the actor who plays the Lord has gone. Find him in his dressing room and tell him that I see him in his own clothes walking a fine line between what was and what could have been. I see him walking on roads I've built and stepping out into woods I remember and cannot shake, however violent a storm brewing in Granny's teapot. Cannot shake Kent. Cannot shake the fear of ghostly monks or The Grey Lady or the sloe or sty or I. There are rows of hops to consider on a bicycle, as Shakespeare's ruffians march forward into history and the dark to act real their wooden swords.

# 60

The point is a wall. A shudder. The other life haunted by the sudden need to draw a line and overstep it. The answer will not be scrawled across a mirror in a recognizable hand. Nothing is visible but wind. To cross the path of your own reflection without being seen is liberty, as in freedom, as in the French Revolution.

The last thought is of pronouns and where they should be placed. Characters do not breathe. Sentences do not resuscitate the dead bodies of a vivid imagination. The glass records nothing; is never for a moment thoughtful or prone to experiment. But there is the girl. She is my last thought. And a pronoun.

She is our first lady's apple in the crotch of our first man. Together they grace the embroiderer's tapestry in comic strip splendour. She is our moment frozen, pleased with itself that it can hang forever over the dark abyss that coughs the rejected sex out.

He is our greatest asset, bending over to kiss our goodnight-daughters with all manner of obscene thought bubbles bending their precious asses in symphony. He is our imagination.

The lights are out all over Eden. Animals are lush and drunk. Bees muffle other bees over the mathematical vista of their own product. It is honey, everyone. The breath of the beasts is thick with liquor and the whole scene is fomenting as she gets up out of her brother's lap and reaches her snaking arm into a mess of leaves.

'It is delicious,' she says.

'Yes, it is delicious. If any fruit is worth the stripping of our former splendour it is this fruit,' he says, shielding what is his from what is hers.

Oh, it is dark! He's behind you! Look behind you! The contents are slop. The deep water and the rock. I want to know if the girl is OK and what she wants to take out of this book when she leaves. Her leather was her bouquet, but I will stitch her a wild mind's eye to replace it.

Joey broods. A sullen, handsome boy on his way to knowing the meaning of the pronoun 'he'. Is a pronoun. Is a word that stands in for another word while that word is busy trying not to be overused.

There is a moment where it looks as if the girl and Joey are going to switch pronouns — like exchanging bracelets or rings, nothing serious, nothing is — but, no, because that would mean taking some White-Out and a cup of tea and going back to my trailer and we're too near the end for that.

# 61

The wall shudders back and rips my hem. I lose the plot to the current. It goes away. I lose the direction of the director. The equipment is turned off. Tired, but well fed, the cast and crew back away from More House laughing and waving. They make the same jokes my parents made about getting rid of us, of me, of me. I don't care!

Only Joey and the girl remain, wearing each other's pronouns in the form of badges of merit. They are pulling my leg. Siamese twins in need of a good sawing.

'We're off, too,' says Joey.

'Thanks for starting us up,' says the girl, my dolly, my peg-doll with her cap of woollen hair.

Joey puts the girl into his pocket. Dead still. Sure she is dead still in her button, her story. And then he grows up, through the roof, a giant vine of promise, laden with peapods, fat and bursting at my mouth. I'm happy. For starters, I'll have peas bursting at their seams with joy. For my main dish, a fig accompanied by a carrot. Nothing complicated. And for dessert, raspberries with cream and sugar. One bowl for me and the other for my grandmother, Dora. Not dead, never dead, still here to tell me what's what and what's next.

## *Acknowledgments*

Thank you to all of you who have listened to me talk about *More House* over the years. Special thanks to Jes Battis, Jeremy Beuhler, David Boulter, Thea Bowering, Connor Byrne, Kirsten Carthew, Stephen Collis, Wayde Compton, Jonathan Crago, Curtis Emde, Mike Hayes, Janet Neigh, Lee Shedden, Glen Stosic, Steven Tan, Sharon Thesen and Cathleen With. Thank you to Michael Barnholden for passing *More House* to Rolf Maurer, to Rolf for choosing to publish it, and to Stefania Alexandru for attending to its production. And thank you to my family: Adrienne, Dylan, Holi, Rueben, Racheal and especially to Sergi, for giving me the space to finish this book.

Mixed Sources
Product group from well-managed
forests and other controlled sources
www.fsc.org Cert no. SGS-COC-2624
© 1996 Forest Stewardship Council
FSC